"Terezia?"

The women murmured excitedly to each other, their voices like bells.

"Duncan? Duncan MacLeod?"

It was Terezia, and he would not greet her on his knees. The blade of the sword bent alarmingly, but held, as he shoved himself upright again.

For a moment he couldn't tell which of the blurred figures before him was hers. They were gathered around chirruping like birds, adjusting the veils over their faces so that only their eyes were exposed. It seemed a great waste of energy, considering how light their clothing was; here, in the safety of their own quarters, they didn't bother with the all-enveloping robes.

One of them wasn't even bothering with the veil. And she had blue eyes, light brown hair, fair pale skin; she was dressed in a thin cotton gown and looked like an angel without the wings. She was looking at him with terror and concern. "Duncan, you're hurt—"

"Ach, no, it's nothing." He smiled. Pulling in a deep breath, he went on, "I came to fetch you out, my lady."

⭕⭕⭕⭕

OTHER BOOKS IN THIS SERIES:

Highlander: Element of Fire

Published by
WARNER BOOKS

HIGHLANDER™

SCIMITAR

ASHLEY McCONNELL

ASPECT®

WARNER BOOKS

A Time Warner Company

WARNER BOOKS EDITION

Copyright © 1996 by Warner Books, Inc.
All rights reserved.

"Highlander" is a protected trademark of Gaumont Television. © 1994 by Gaumont Television and © Davis Panzer Productions, Inc. 1985.
Published by arrangement with Bohbot Entertainment, Inc.

Aspect is a registered trademark of Warner Books, Inc.

Warner Books, Inc.
1271 Avenue of the Americas
New York, NY 10020

Ⓦ A Time Warner Company

Printed in the United States of America

First Printing: February, 1996

10 9 8 7 6 5 4 3 2 1

AUTHOR'S NOTES AND ACKNOWLEDGEMENTS

The first part of *Scimitar* is based, of course, on the Algiers flashback in Part I of the third season Finale of HIGHLANDER. Particular thanks are due to David Tynan, whose script it is; to Gillian Horvath and Donna Lettow, for providing the flashback details; and to Shirley Emin, who mentioned the Barbary corsairs at the right moment.

The second part of the book is *very* loosely based on the Arab Revolt, and is set in the last month of 1916 and the early part of 1917. Several of the people named, including T. E. Lawrence (who later came to be known as Lawrence of Arabia), Colonel Clayton, and the Emir Faisal ibn Hussein, are real. Faisal's army was indeed progressing up the coast of the Red Sea during this time. Petra is a real place, and my thanks go to Richard Halliburton for recording the "rose-red city, half as old as time," in his *Book of Marvels.*

Everything else, particularly the tribes of Rushallah and the Irzed and the legendary treasure house, is a product of my own imagination, with the help of Nina Kiriki Hoffman's magic sprinkles.

Additional thanks should go to Sean Antonio Romero, who provided the sourcebook for more research material on the martial arts than I could possibly use here, and to Betsy Mitchell, who took a *great* deal on faith and handled a sensitive situation with tact and humor.

Any historical or linguistic errors are, of course, entirely my own responsibility.

HIGHLANDER™

SCIMITAR

Prologue: The Watcher

A Watcher was supposed to Watch: observe, record, report. That meant putting forth some effort from time to time, Joe Dawson acknowledged. He'd gotten lazy, though, since the subject of the Watching knew about it. Sometimes he even talked to Joe about his life. It had made Joe's job much simpler.

But as usual, when a job got too simple, details got easier to overlook. He was reminded he'd been neglecting his duties when the package arrived at the bar, and he couldn't recall the last time he'd had a conversation with its intended recipient.

Someone had left it sitting there, one afternoon in early June, before the evening crowd began wandering in. He couldn't figure out how the thing got there; one minute the bar was empty, the next the box was lying on the corner of the stage, next to a guitar case. The package wasn't small, either: a good four feet long, a foot wide, some six inches deep, wrapped up in brown paper and tied with twine, a cream-colored business card tucked under the knot. A name was written on the card in flowing brown ink. Joe hefted the parcel: not too heavy. Nothing ticked ominously.

The bartender was new, still learning where the good stuff was kept, and he swore there hadn't been anyone there. Joe merely cocked an ironic eye at him, snorted, and decided it was time to go visiting.

Watching.

Keeping track.

Leaning on his cane in the doorway of the dojo, he watched Duncan MacLeod move through the elegant, deadly forms of a kata, sweat glistening on his upper body. Light gleamed on the blade of the sword shrieking through the air, left shimmering afterimages that hurt the eyes. MacLeod's face was very still, his attention focused inward. His movement was a cross between dance and death.

He looked like a man who had spent most of a lifetime in such exercise. He was tall, appeared to be in his midthirties; sleek-muscled, with long dark hair tied back in a ponytail that whipped the air as he spun and leaped, shadowfighting. The elegant grace of it gave the Watcher an unaccustomed pang of envy, a feeling of weariness in his bones, a sense that he was—getting old.

That was ironic, too. Joe brushed at his graying beard and smiled to himself. Anyone looking at the two of them together might be forgiven for thinking him perhaps twenty years older than the man who fought with shadows.

The rest of the dojo was empty at this hour, the exercise mats rolled up neatly out of the way. The weapons were racked or mounted, as if they were no more than conversation pieces, works of art interrupting the bare starkness of the walls.

The exercise was complete, finished with a snapped nod, a silent salute to the invisible opponent. Joe stifled an urge to applaud. He did shift his weight, and MacLeod pivoted smoothly, unstartled.

"Joe. Hello." A faint, pleasant accent, too light to identify anymore, flavored his voice. A glint of pleased recognition lit his dark eyes.

"You're slipping, MacLeod. You don't want somebody sneaking up on you one day."

The words were wry, and the man to whom they were addressed met them with an equally wry smile in response. It wouldn't happen—not now, not ever. Joe was reasonably sure MacLeod had known someone was standing in the doorway in the same heartbeat he had arrived; focus on the kata notwithstanding, MacLeod was always aware of his environment.

Now, setting the sword aside, he reached for a towel and began to dry the sweat from his chest and arms. "Something up?" he asked, perhaps a trifle too casually.

"No, no. Just hadn't seen you for a few days, thought I'd look in and see how you were doing." Joe moved away from the doorway, limping over to look at the sword. It was a practice weapon, weighted to duplicate another weapon, kept out of sight but always to hand. He shifted the package under one arm, mentally measuring the sword against it.

MacLeod chuckled. "I'm doing fine, Joe. No ancient enemies showing up, no new ones either. It's quiet. I like it that way." He tossed the towel over his shoulder, led the other man into the back office of the dojo.

This, too, showed much of the spare good taste of its owner. Weapons hung on these walls as well, but this was a room for doing business, with a wooden desk—not expensive, but not cheap either—office chairs, and metal file cabinets. It was a place where work was done, and clutter was not permitted.

A bottle of water waited on the desk; MacLeod took it up and drank deeply, ostentatiously not looking at the package Dawson carried under his arm. Dawson waited; MacLeod was in excellent shape and would recover quickly from the exercise, and then there were the private rituals of friendship to be observed.

Thirst satisfied, MacLeod pulled on a white T-shirt that had been draped neatly over the back of his chair, and opened a drawer in the desk. He produced a bottle of single-malt whisky and two glasses. Pouring a fingerful into each glass, he handed one to Joe and raised the other. "To peace and quiet."

Joe acknowledged the toast and took a sip of the liquid, holding it in his mouth a moment before swallowing. MacLeod raised his eyebrows, waiting.

Dawson took his time, considering. Finally he said, "This is, ah, let's see. Dark Roses? That little place up near Inverness."

MacLeod grinned. "Right. I thought I'd had you there."

The Watcher grinned back. "It's all right." He took another sip.

"Not bad," MacLeod agreed, looking critically at the contents of the glass. "I've had worse." Setting the glass aside, he reached for a long-sleeved shirt and shrugged it on, dropping the towel on the desk as he did so, plopping himself into the desk chair and swiveling around to face his visitor. "So. What's the real reason?"

Joe lowered himself stiffly into the visitor's chair, setting the package on the desk. "Just say hello, that's all. Oh, and there's this." He indicated the box.

The other man examined it curiously. "What's this?"

"Somebody left it for you at the bar. We didn't see who left it; the new day guy isn't too bright."

MacLeod turned over the card with his name on it, looking in vain for a message on the back. It was blank.

He shrugged, tossing the card back on the desk, and poured himself just enough more whisky to cover the bottom of the glass.

"Aren't you going to open it?"

MacLeod finished his drink. "Nah. It'll keep." He burst out laughing at the expression of disappointment that crossed the other man's face. "All right, all right. Is it your birthday or something?" Pulling the package back, he yanked the twine apart with casual strength and ripped the paper away.

Torn away, the paper revealed a large plain case, rectangular, with rounded corners, of some old, highly polished dark wood that shone almost with a life of its own; the brass hinges were tinged faintly green with age. There was no lock. The lid was shallow, a quarter the depth of the whole thing. It appeared to be more formal than a mere box: rather, it appeared to be a case specifically designed for something, something long and flat and narrow. Like one of the weapons on the wall.

"What is it?"

MacLeod's hand hovered at the corner, as if reluctant to lift the lid. He had, Joe realized suddenly, the same introspective look on his face that it had worn earlier, when he was moving through the meditative forms of the exercise. He sat back to watch, fascinated, wondering what MacLeod was thinking, what he was remembering. It was obvious that he recognized the container.

Joe wanted, very badly, to ask again what the thing was, what it contained, what memories it triggered. He suspected that he knew, but suspicion wasn't enough; he was supposed to know. It was his business, after all. He was a Watcher; Duncan MacLeod was his assigned subject.

But there was more to their relationship than that. Duncan MacLeod was his friend, as well. So he kept silent, refusing to intrude, knowing that his curiosity would be satisfied eventually.

MacLeod's fingers drifted over the glossy wood, as if caressing it, and then, as if he had reached a sudden decision, he set the wooden case back on the desk and flipped back the lid to display the contents.

"My God!" The Watcher was unable to restrain his surprise. He rose to his feet, leaning over to get a closer look.

The box held a scimitar, a long curved blade set in a worn black leather scabbard. At first glance it didn't appear particularly prepossessing; it was inlaid with no rubies or emeralds, no enamel on the guard. The sword had a hilt of plain rough silver, bent back at a right angle, with a ring set where the pommel should be. The scabbard, too, was decorated for part of its length with silver, worked in a fine embroidered wire.

Then MacLeod took the hilt in his hand and slid it free of the cracked and dusty leather, lifted the sword up to the light.

The damascened blue-gray metal shone like triumph, catching the light in ripples, as if the steel was viewed through water, or oil. Along the back, near the hilt, the blade had been chiseled out in arabesques and inlaid with gold; along its length, more gold inlay set off an inscription in flowing Arabic characters.

Joe drew a reverent breath. "That's beautiful."

"Yes," MacLeod agreed absently. He rose, stepped away from the desk, and slashed at the air, his wrist twisting. He put his back into it; the blade shrieked as if it had a life of its own, and stopped a fraction of an inch from the chair. He raised it again, inspecting the edge, and ran his thumb along it.

Joe winced as blood welled up and ran down the metal. MacLeod cursed, sucking at the cut and setting the sword down, carefully, to reach for a soft cloth.

The cloth wasn't for the cut. The cut, in fact, was almost gone by the time the man removed his thumb from his mouth, and he dried saliva and leftover blood on the leg of his jeans and took up the sword again to clean away the red stain on the blade.

Joe had seen this before, a hundred times, and it still sent a chill through him. The cut had been deep, to the bone; enough blood had flowed to run clear to the base of the man's thumb; now there was no sign of it. MacLeod didn't appear even to notice. He was polishing the blade with slow, even, practiced strokes. The muscles in the corner of his mouth tightened in what might have been a reminiscent smile.

He obviously knew the weapon. The polishing was a welcoming of an old acquaintance, a smoothing away of years of separation. From the expression on his face, the scimitar represented both good memories and painful ones.

"How old is it?" Joe asked, very quietly. He could see, now, that the inlaid inscription was so worn down in places as to be illegible; the enameling had chipped out in two places. There was a dent in the hilt. The silver was badly tarnished, nearly black in places.

"I don't know," MacLeod said thoughtfully, still absorbed in the polishing. "At lest three hundred and fifty years. Someone's making me a very nice gift."

"You've been looking for it, then?"

"No, not really. I'm glad to have it, though." He looked up, past his visitor, as if searching for the right spot on the wall.

"Whose was it?"

"It belonged to one of my very first teachers," MacLeod said. "He was a good man."

That was one of the good memories, Joe could tell. As well as one of the painful ones.

And how, he wondered, could someone like MacLeod untangle them, after so many years? More than four hundred—how many swords had he seen in four hundred years?

Joe blinked. For a moment the man sitting across the table from him was something other, something more than just Duncan MacLeod, sometime owner of a dojo and an antique store, world traveler, occasional raconteur, good man, loyal friend, connoisseur of single-malt whiskies.

He was an Immortal. He had been born in the Highlands more than four hundred years ago, and he could not die unless someone took his head, and with it his power.

Joe Dawson knew all this intellectually—it was why he Watched, after all—but sometimes, as now, it hit him in the gut that he would never truly understand what it was like to carry centuries worth of memories, to take another Immortal's head and with it the Quickening, to watch as the world changed, as time passed and mortals died. Dawson might *feel* old, watching MacLeod; but generations of men like Joe Dawson had passed away while this scimitar and this man remained. It was no wonder the glistening steel evoked such a bond in him.

"It's not a message, then?"

MacLeod shook his head. "If it is, I don't know what it might be." He smiled suddenly. "It doesn't matter, though. Someone who knows me, and knows—this." He touched the blade again, lightly.

Now Joe was even more curious. But it wasn't polite to grill his host, and when MacLeod put the sword aside the conversation turned to ordinary things, current events, politics, sports, women, music, all the things ordinary men, friends, might have talked about in a long June evening. They might have been anywhere at all, much less in a martial-arts studio.

It was late when the Watcher finally returned home. He put on an old blues album and went to his journal, intending to update his records with a short paragraph. Watching an Immortal often meant periods of great boredom punctuated by short periods of dreadful activity. Once the task was finished, he replaced the leather-bound book on the shelf beside the rest. All the records were stored on disk as well; but Joe found he preferred the sensory feel of the volumes themselves.

They were all alike, those books: they'd been rebound over the centuries, sometimes copied and translated, the better to preserve their contents. Most, though, were originals, passed down generations to rest for the time being with him. The covers were marked with the same symbol he had tattooed on his wrist, the trefoil-in-circles.

These two dozen volumes were the records of Watcher and Watched, over centuries—not just the life of Duncan MacLeod, but of others Joe Dawson had Watched play and lose the Game, and their heads. He'd been quite fond of some of them, in a remote sort of way. He'd never been friends with one before.

The gift of the sword still nagged at him. To an Immortal, it had to carry special meaning; he wondered what sort of memories it might represent.

His eyes narrowed as he looked at the records again.

An Arab sword.

Three hundred and fifty years.

Where was Duncan MacLeod three hundred and fifty years ago? He'd barely been Immortal a single lifetime, back then. He'd been—just where *had* he been, that he could have crossed paths with an Arab sword, belonging to one of his first teachers?

Thoughtfully, he reached for one of the first books, one worn and battered, the leather dry and dusty. He opened it carefully, thinking he should take better care of the record of a life, and began to read, puzzling out the awkward, faded writing, the words in old and unfamiliar languages.

Chapter One

*In the year of Our Lord 1653, in the Doge's blessed
city of Venice. The Scots Immortal has parted
company from this city in peace, for which God be
thanked. MacLeod takes ship from Venice for Spain.
It is an ill time to travel; the Turks are insolent. I
shall send messages by pigeon to my fellows along
the way. In the meantime, I prepare to accompany
MacLeod. Never let it be said that I have failed my
calling and betrayed my oath.*

—Ignatius Bell'domo

For the first time since he had died thirty years before, Duncan MacLeod wished, profoundly, that he had stayed dead. Doubled over the side of a Venetian sailing ship, he tried once again to bring forth something, anything, out of his queasy stomach, but there was nothing left except nausea.

Meanwhile the life and business of the *Sancta Innocenta* continued unconcernedly about him. The sailors had long since lost interest in making jokes about the tall, well-dressed man with the dreadful accent and no sea legs. The other passengers, fortunately, still eyed him with some sympathy.

"You know, people do get used to it," said one, slapping him on the back in friendly fashion.

MacLeod looked around at him blearily. He was too weak, at the moment, to do murder, though the idea was very tempting. The ship rose and fell with the long swell of the Mediterranean waves, and MacLeod's vision swam with the fishes.

"You lie," he gasped out, his Italian thick with the burr of Scotland. "No one could get used to this. Holy God, does it never stop *moving*?"

The other man laughed. "Oh, I used to be as bad as you. Now I rather like it. You *will* live through it, I promise."

Alfonso d'Valenzuela never knew how close he came to death in that moment; if he had been an Immortal, MacLeod would have taken the man's head with his teeth. Except, of course, that the thought of swallowing blood made him retch again.

"Ah, my poor brave Duncan," came a woman's voice from behind him. "Has the sea defeated you?"

He closed his eyes and rested his forehead on the railing. "Not yet."

It was supposed to be a growl. It came out sounding as miserable as he felt. Eventually he managed to pull himself more or less upright to squint wearily over the gently rolling horizon. He would not, *not* heave again, he swore it. His jaw was clenched against the possibility. He was no puling boy, he was a man, and to be sick this way, particularly under the eyes of a woman, was shameful. Turning to glance behind him, he caught sight of her and smiled wanly, grateful for the distraction of the sight of her. Yes, it was especially humiliating to be sick before such a woman as Terezia, just sixteen, high-spirited, with a complexion like milk, her lips like cherries . . . he bolted for the rail again.

"Oh, dear." A light hand lifted his chin, and a damp cloth wiped at his face. He looked down blearily to see Terezia herself industriously scrubbing at his cheek and chin, her elegant eyebrows knit with concentration. She showed not the slightest sign of distress at the mess he'd made of himself.

It was one of the most endearing things about her, he'd decided months ago. Even in the Doge's court Terezia d'Alessandro, under the watchful eye of her father, her brother Gioninno, and her guardsman d'Valenzuela, mixed freely with the merchants and ambassadors and nobility from all the courts of Europe and the East. She showed no more dismay at sharing a table with a Muslim lord from the Sublime Porte in Constantinople than she did in discussing love poetry with an English merchant—less, in fact, but then the Englishman was a boor.

In the shadowed, perfumed halls of the Doge's palace Terezia had laughed and flirted and captured his heart with a teasing kiss, and he had fallen a little in love with her. She had made it clear that a kiss was all he would have of her, a kiss and a dance and a smile.

And now, a cloth to wash away his sickness and make him feel better.

Duncan finally regained enough equilibrium to catch at her wrist. "That's enough, lass. I thank you."

She smiled at him. "I'm sorry you don't travel well, Duncan. I think traveling the sea is so wonderful." The Mediterranean Sea was the blue of sapphires, with a lining of white on each wave. Sunlight glittered on the water. Gulls tilted back and forth on the warm salt breeze, calling. It was quite beautiful, of course, much as a landscape filled with jewels, much as the woman at his side was beautiful, but it would keep *moving* so. . . .

"Ah, well." He reached behind him to take a surreptitious deathgrip on the rail. "Best you go back to your father, now. We wouldn't want him to get the wrong idea. As for the sea— Perhaps your new husband will take you with him sometimes."

"My . . . new husband. Yes." She smiled again, and winked, and swayed away to stand beside her father, who was glowering at the exchange. Something about her expression bothered the Highlander. He hoped she hadn't decided she was going to run away with her bodyguard. She was a good girl, really, perhaps too outgoing; she had spent a *lot* of time talking to the Turkish ambassadors. But she was never scandalous. D'Valenzuela had always been nearby, or her father, or Duncan, keeping an eye on her. Still, it was no secret she didn't want this marriage, to a trading partner of her father's in Spain.

The *Sancta Innocenta* was a decent-sized, if old, galley flying the flag of Venice. The twin masts were supplemented by a bank of oars for maneuvering when the wind failed. She carried six passengers, a cargo of silk and tea from Cathay, and a substantial dowry in gold and jewels. The entire cargo belonged to the Signore d'Alessandro.

Besides the family d'Alessandro was another, secretive little man calling himself Calizione, who kept himself apart; Duncan had been too seasick to find out any more about him. And then there was Duncan MacLeod himself, who was there because the *Sancta Innocenta* was lifting anchor when the impulse struck him to go. He had met the d'Alessandros at one of the huge banquets the Doge gave, where persons of all nations and importance met, conversed, dealt secretly with one another. He had gotten to know them and d'Valenzuela in several such encounters. He had been delighted to accept the invitation to accompany them, adding his sword to Alfonso's for the protection of them all.

At least, he had been delighted until the ship had cleared the harbor. Even the English Channel had not made him as sick as the deceptively gentle Mediterranean. From the first day out, he had been ill to some degree. Terezia had clucked over him like a worried bantam hen, much to the amusement of everyone else.

They had moved around the boot of Italy and were making the long run to Spain, hoping to avoid arousing the unwelcome attention of the Turkish corsairs. With the Knights no longer in Malta, every fishing boat was regarded with suspicion, and the captain was feeling particularly uneasy. His crew was mostly Spanish, and he was headed to a Spanish port; it was as good as a bonfire to attract the attention of pirates. There had to be an excellent reason, such as the cementing of a trade alliance or the profit of a good cargo, to risk venturing out.

MacLeod knew all this; it had been common talk at court. Still, his innate restlessness was enough to drive him on. Every day, now, he realized again what it meant to be thirty-one years past his own death. Back home, the men he had played with as a boy were dying of old age, while he remained young and strong, never changing. Someday, he thought, he'd be used to it. As yet, he was not.

So he did things impulsively. He took ship for Spain for no other reason than that he was tired of Venice and the tide was going. Somewhere there would be a battle, somewhere someone would hire his sword and he could experience again what it was like to die without dying, risk without risking anything really important. He was Immortal.

His friend d'Valenzuela was not. He was merely a decent drinking companion (if one liked sweet wine), with a decent sense of humor about him as long as he wasn't talking about *mal de mer*. He was there to stand escort and keep Gioninno out of trouble.

The boy was forever clambering about the rigging, from which uneasy perch he insisted upon looking for Turkish ships. Three times in two days he had caused a small panic with false sightings, until the captain, in an apoplectic fit, ordered him down. The only thing keeping him from being thrown to the fishes, MacLeod thought, was his father's share in the cargo. Even more annoying than Gioninno's puppylike enthusiasm for pirates was his utter lack of reaction to the shifting, heaving, eternally restless sea.

And then there was Terezia. Sweet Terezia, standing at the railing and looking over the sea as if she were without a care in the world. Duncan slumped back against a convenient bulkhead and contemplated her: as free of seasickness as her brother, a vision of loveliness he could appreciate even as his gut churned: her lovely dark eyes, her slender waist, her little hands, so soft against his forehead. She had been kind to him in his misery, even though he could tell that beneath her carefree smile she was harboring tension of her own.

It was the strain of being so far from home, of looking forward to the marriage, he thought charitably, and he could gain merit himself by giving her something else to think about. If only he didn't have to disgrace himself in the doing!

"MacLeod!" It was Gioninno. "You promised to tell me again about the barbarians of your homeland!"

MacLeod glared at him, resenting the distraction.

Oblivious, Gioninno grabbed him by the arm and pulled him away from the bulkhead, back toward the rail. The deck rose and fell under Duncan's feet, and he crumbled, clinging to a handy line. Gioninno paid no heed. "Tell me again. I thought the Stuart was a Scot?"

"Aye. Or so he claims." The Immortal attempted to rise from the deck and moaned to himself as his stomach tried to turn inside out.

"So you Scots conquered the barbaric English after all. It is most romantic." Gioninno nodded with great satisfaction. "A pity, though, that it could not have been in glorious battle. It is much better to win in battle, is it not?"

"Oh, aye." MacLeod's head was throbbing, too. Perhaps it was the plague. Unfortunately, he couldn't die permanently of the plague, either, or so he had been taught. He wondered if he could rig up a blade to fall upon him and end this misery—

"The roar of battle! The clash of arms! The music of the trumpets!" Gioninno waxed ecstatic, carried away by his own visions.

MacLeod, whose memories of battle ran more to the smell of blood and ordure and the screams of dying men, only shook his head. Glory, yes, there was always glory to be won by a strong sword arm, and wealth; he could sympathize with the boy's excitement. At the moment, however, he was losing his battle with the sea once more, and he felt anything but glorious. Launching himself for the deck rail, he draped himself over it just in time.

Gioninno followed, gamboling at MacLeod's heels like a half-grown puppy.

"Leave him be, boy," Alfonso advised from his place near the mast. "Have some mercy, after all."

"Oh, Signor MacLeod is only suffering from a most minor upset," Gioninno responded, waving off the suggestion. "Look, the fishing ships are moving off— Look! It's a xebec! A Turkish ship!"

"Holy Mother of God, boy—" Alfonso said wearily. "I thought you tired of that yesterday."

But Gioninno was climbing onto the railing in his excitement, and MacLeod peered up, blinking to clear his vision. On the near horizon he saw a low-hulled, single-masted ship. It was coming directly for them.

He straightened to see better, the nausea receding some-what.

From the rigging came a sudden shout, as the watchman belatedly caught sight of the xebec.

The rest of the crew took up the cry.

"God's blood! They *are* corsairs!" Alfonso was at the rail too, staring at the other ship. Behind them stood d'Alessandro and his lovely daughter.

The next few minutes were frantic with activity, as the *Sancta Innocenta* rigged for escape or battle. The captain shouted hoarse orders and the crew boiled across the deck like bees from a kicked hive, raising sail.

It was close enough now to see the faces of the crew of the xebec, faces dark and light, all grinning ferociously with the mad glee of men going into battle. A figure in the bow shouted a command for the *Sancta Innocenta* to heave to. A row of brass cannon slid out through the ports as the xebec came about, bringing its guns to bear.

"What is he doing?" Gioninno yelped.

"He's getting ready to fire on us if we don't surrender," Alfonso snapped. "Get away from that rail, boy. Get down below, or you'll find your head blown off."

MacLeod jerked around, startled, instinctively reaching for his sword. His nausea receded abruptly as more important matters took precedence.

"Wait until they board," Alfonso recommended, loosening his own rapier.

"They're fair close for cannon, are they not?" MacLeod said. "Are they mad?" Small boats, loaded with screaming warriors of all colors from night-black to reddened ivory, danced across the water.

"No—they're boarding," Alfonso said. "Damn you, Gioninno, Terezia, get you below. You're in the way."

"Duncan," she whispered. "You will be careful, won't you? The holy saints will take care of us."

"Get below," he snapped. The holy saints weren't providing enough firepower to make a difference at the moment.

The two ships were side to side now. The boats were too low and too close for the *Sancta Innocenta* to fire upon. The Venetian ship's captain was screaming hoarsely at his men, yelling at them to put on sail, to whip the oarsmen to greater effort. Twenty or so sailors abandoned the lines to scurry for knives. The captain, standing on the poop deck, shouted orders as he fumbled to load a brace of pistols.

There was nothing for MacLeod to do but wait. The two ships wallowed in the heavy seas, maneuvering for advantage. One of the cannons roared, and the deck shuddered under the Scotsman's feet.

Meanwhile, corsairs lowered more boats from the xebec and rowed themselves across beneath the cannons, carrying knives and swords between their teeth. Burned dark by the sun, they were dressed in diaperlike cloths rolled about their loins and nothing else.

Gioninno shoved himself in front of MacLeod and d'Valenzuela, flailing a rapier and posing heroically. Scotsman and Spaniard exchanged exasperated glances and simultaneously reached out for the boy's shoulders, pushing him back into the arms of his hysterical father.

The pirates threw hooks to the rail of the ship and swarmed aboard, screaming, ululating, brandishing swords, intent upon overwhelming the passengers and crew of the *Sancta Innocenta* with the mass of their flesh and the terror of their aspect. The waiting was over. The enemy came in waves.

They were met by desperation—and a mad Scot. It was more resistance than the corsairs were prepared for. MacLeod lost himself in the battle madness, the smell of blood and gunpowder thick in his nostrils, the splintering of wood and the screams of metal and dying men sharp in his ears. His arm ached from the endless swing and cut and thrust of the heavy sword. Everything else was forgotten in the sudden passion of battle, of killing; the rise and fall of the ship became a part of MacLeod, aiding his arm as he feinted and parried and men died before him.

But it was a lost battle, and he knew it from the beginning. Even the captain lost heart quickly. Such battles were too common; ships would be taken, ransomed, over and over. . . . The crew, which chose slavery and the hope of escape to the certain death of continuing the fight, ended paralyzed by fear and huddled into a circle around the mast. The rest of the corsairs closed around the last knot of resistance: the merchants and the boy, MacLeod and d'Valenzuela.

The discreet little stranger Calizione pushed his way from behind the wall of MacLeod's and d'Valenzuela's shoulders, his hands clutching a bag of gold, pushing it at the grinning pirates, babbling of ransom. The leader snatched it from his hands, pulled the strings loose with his teeth, and looked inside. His grin even wider, he shouted something to his fellows. The merchant nodded hysterically, promising more of the same.

The pirate laughed and swung his arm, and the merchant's head, its mouth still opening and closing, went rolling across the deck, while the body swayed in place and then toppled down in front of MacLeod like a fallen tree.

He watched the body fall with a cold horror. There was no Quickening—the man hadn't been Immortal—but decapitation took mortals too. He looked up to meet the pirate's eyes, saw laughter, saw the man react to his own reaction.

He struck, as much to wipe out that recognition of his own fear as to eliminate any threat, and the man dropped under the thrust and came up inside his guard, knocking his sword aside. At the same time d'Valenzuela screamed as another pirate slashed him across the upper part of his thigh. The two of them were borne down under the weight of their opponents, and the sword was torn out of MacLeod's hand.

He struggled still, frantic to regain his weapon, until someone got leverage to strike him across the temple, and the world turned gray.

He could feel hands upon him, tearing at his clothing; he could hear voices, as if from very far away, shouting in a multitude of languages—Italian curses, Spanish moans, French imprecations, even a sentence or two in English, as well as a steady stream of something that might be Turkish, or Arabic, or Berber. Or perhaps all three; he couldn't tell, didn't care.

After a long, muzzy time, he became aware of the roughness of wood pressed against his cheek, the stink of fish and humans and the sea, the thickness of blood in his mouth. As awareness returned, the consequences of injury faded with the injury itself. He resisted the urge to lift his head and look around, keeping his eyes shut and using his other senses instead.

He wasn't bound. That was the first thing.

He could hear the familiar creak of wood and rope, the snap of sails. The orders shouted from one end of the ship to another were no longer in Italian, though. A prize crew had taken over.

He could hear Gioninno's voice, raised in querulous protest, and his father, attempting without success to silence him. He couldn't hear anyone else close.

He could feel the salt breeze against his skin.

Drawing in a deep breath, he finally opened his eyes, turned his head.

They were still where they had fallen, outside the cabin door. Gioninno and his father were huddled together, stripped to their breeches, looking foolish and pale against the dark wood of the cabin and deck. Another form lay slack against the cabin, stripped too, an open wound in his leg oozing blood in a pool around the bottom half of his body. Flies crawled over and into the injury.

He raised himself up, slowly, to a sitting position, and looked farther afield. His first instinct was to look for the girl, but Terezia was nowhere in sight. He could see members of the prize crew, wearing bits and pieces of clothing he recognized—including his own shirt and boots. A half-dozen of them were sitting on the deck, casting dice for his belt and d'Valenzuela's necklace. None of them seemed to be particularly concerned with their prisoners, unbound and free.

On the other hand, MacLeod acknowledged with grim humor, there wasn't anywhere they could go. He stood up, and the pirates gave him a few casual glances and went on with their business.

D'Valenzuela was unconscious. MacLeod batted the flies away, looked about for something to bind the wound.

"He's going to die," the merchant said spitefully. "He's Spanish. They're Moors, they hate the Spanish."

MacLeod glanced at the polyglot pirate crew. "Wise of you to hire him, then. Where's your daughter?"

"They took her below, to keep her separate, away from the crew." D'Alessandro wiped at his forehead. "They haven't hurt her; she's worth more to them that way." He sounded like a man trying to give himself courage. "They're all corsairs. Muslim, renegade Christian— They're taking us to Algiers. They'll sell us for slaves."

"I'm no slave." MacLeod looked over the wound. It was already beginning to fester in the heat, and he could see eggs from the flies. He was no surgeon, but he'd seen enough battle to know that unless something was done immediately, d'Valenzuela would lose the leg, if not his life.

"I need wine, and bandages."

"You're mad. He's going to die."

"Damn your eyes, I want bandages!"

The merchant backed up against the wall, trying to get away from the raging madman lunging at him. The yell, and the merchant's squawk of dismay, attracted the attention of the captain of the prize crew.

"What goes on here?" It was atrocious Italian. Even MacLeod, whose Italian was still rough with the burr of the Highlands, winced at the sound of it.

Unlike the rest of his crew, the man was dressed in red satin pantaloons and a white silk shirt, torn and bloody from the fight, with an equally filthy white turban. He had three knives and a large pistol stuck in his belt. He wore an earring of beaten gold in his ear, so heavy the lobe was dragged down and open, and a tangle of necklaces. His beard, oddly, was trimmed short. It was hard to tell where he came from originally; he was burned dark from the endless sun, and certainly the accent gave no hint.

"What is this noise? Is the man dead?"

MacLeod gave him a considering stare; he was twice the man's size, he could kill him without appreciable effort.

"Not yet," he said evenly. "I need wine, and bandages."

The corsair looked casually at the recumbent body, waved over a pair of his men nearby. "He's close enough to dead already. Throw him overboard."

MacLeod rose to his feet. "No."

The sailors paused, looking to their leader.

The corsair and the Scot stared at each other.

"Where's the profit to you, man, if he dies?" MacLeod went on, ignoring the pirates. "He's Spanish. Aye, you hate all the sons of Spain, but his family will ransom him. Nobody pays gold for a dead man." He kept his voice quiet, reasonable. He might be willing and able to kill the man, if only to wipe the sneer from his face, but that wouldn't save Alfonso. Or Terezia.

The corsair captain sneered. "Nobody would pay gold for the likes of him. He's not worth it. Throw him overboard."

The pirates moved in.

Duncan grabbed an arm. "Wait."

The other man paused in the act of turning away. "What, then?" he asked, impatient.

"*I'll* buy his life."

The captain looked at MacLeod, standing half-naked and empty-handed, and laughed. Around him, the other pirates laughed too, the pool spreading as those who understood translated the offer for those who didn't.

"And what will you pay us with?" the captain inquired. "Have we overlooked something, infidel?"

"You're mad," the merchant hissed. "Completely mad. I don't know you, I want nothing to do with you—Nino, come away from him—"

"I'll fight you for him." He had nothing else to offer, really. They had taken all he had, and he hadn't had much to begin with.

"Why should I do such a thing?" the captain said, folding himself down to balance on the balls of his feet. "You're nothing, infidel. You have nothing. What would you buy him with?"

"Honor, perhaps. More honor than thieves have."

It took the pirate captain aback, and he glanced at d'Valenzuela again. The wounded man stirred and moaned, as if he knew his fate was the subject of the discussion. "This man, he means something to you? He is your brother?"

"He's a friend."

"And you will fight for him, you say. If you win, we give you wine, bandages. If you lose?"

"Then you can throw me to the fishes with him." For a

moment MacLeod regretted the answer. It was too easy an offer for an Immortal to make.

He couldn't help it, though, if he couldn't die. That wasn't his fault.

Compelling honesty made him add, "Or you could take my head, if you had any use for it." If he was going to invoke honor, in the name of the Clan MacLeod he'd do so honorably. There were no other Immortals on board, but if his head came away from his body, he'd die anyway.

One of the corsairs made a remark to another, and a second roar of laughter went up. MacLeod didn't need any translation to know what they were saying, and he held his temper in check with an effort; it would do no good to add fuel to that fire. Another pirate yelled something to his captain, and the man responded with something else that made the rest of them laugh. In the back of the crowd, men started talking to each other in the way that meant the world over that bets were being exchanged. MacLeod allowed himself a breath of hope.

The captain knew it too. He looked over his crew, and at the crew of the *Sancta Innocenta*, who were intent on the betting too, and shrugged. "Well, fool. It might be amusing." He grinned again. "But you need an opponent nearer your own size for such a match. Murak!"

MacLeod turned to see more movement among the crew, and they parted to make way for the summoned man.

From the name, he expected to see another Moor, or perhaps a Sudanese, one of the dark men who turned up occasionally in the European ports. What he did not expect was a huge man, with no sign of fat anywhere on his body; a man with bronzed skin, long hair knotted at the nape of his neck, and long blond mustaches tied back behind his head. His feet were bare, his breeches ragged, and he was as shirtless as MacLeod himself, revealing a massive chest covered by swirling tattoos in blue and red and yellow. He dragged a long, stone-headed club on the deck as he came. He looked like a German out of Caesar's own nightmares.

"This is Murak," the captain said conversationally. "It's well you should know who will kill you, Scot. Murak has heard the names of fifty men, and they all died. Tell him who you are, so he knows who is the fifty-first."

"I am Duncan MacLeod of the Clan MacLeod," he answered absentmindedly, more interested in studying his opponent than in declaring his genealogy. "Are we agreed, then? If I beat him, d'Valenzuela will get good care?"

"Oh, yes. We are agreed." The teeth remaining to the captain glinted in the sun. "And if he beats you, you are both dead."

"You cannot kill me."

"Arrogant," the captain said, as the audience scattered for the rail, and Murak's club swung unannounced through the air, straight for MacLeod's head.

Chapter Two

*In the one thousand and thirty-first year of the
Hegira, the flight of our holy prophet Mohammed,
blessed be he: The infidel Scottish Immortal is held
captive by my lord Abdul ibn Rais. My fellow
Watcher lies dead. I take up his duty, as is required
of me.*

—Hamid Alat

MacLeod ducked and dodged out into the open deck, looking
frantically for a weapon. Murak laughed and swished the
club through the air, taunting him. MacLeod spun and
ducked again; unless the German literally beat his head off,
he'd survive the encounter, but the interval—and the recov-
ery from the damage inflicted in it—was likely to be excruci-
atingly painful.

Besides, being hunted like a rat from one side of the ship
to the other, followed by a crowd of yelling, cheering corsairs and captive crew, was hardly his idea of an honorable
fight. Cursing under his breath, he scrambled out of the way
of yet another blow, and then his glance fell on a short sword
thrust into a belt.

He barreled into the man, knocking him to the deck, and

clawed at the hilt. Armed at last, he turned to face his tormentor.

The sword was shorter than any he had ever seen, and curved almost as a half-moon; his hand was almost too big for the hilt. It was a toy of a weapon, compared to his good broadsword, but Murak stepped back warily when MacLeod swung it, experimentally slicing the air.

It sang. For all its lack of size, the blade was well balanced, well sharpened. Not made for thrusting, the sword led his arm through cuts and parries, and Murak gave way.

But the club gave the bigger man the advantage of even greater reach, and he swung again, now aiming at MacLeod's arm instead of his head. The crowd screamed with glee as the head of the club connected on the flat of the blade, nearly knocking it from MacLeod's hand. The Scot tried to swing the weapon two-handed, as he would his broadsword, but it was too small and light for that. Murak giggled at the sight.

"Stand and fight," the corsair captain yelled. "Fight, Scotsman, or we throw your friend to the sea."

"Aye," MacLeod said between his teeth. "I'm trying." Dropping to one knee, under the arc of the club's swing, he slashed at the other man's legs. Murak screamed and staggered, lines of red blossoming across his legs, and the club came down on MacLeod's sword arm.

He grunted, feeling the bones break and crunch against each other, and the sword rattled onto the deck from his loosened grip. Murak wobbled above him, a mountain of muscle and bone threatening to crash into him, and he scrabbled for the weapon with his other hand, sweeping it up in time to see it slide gracefully into the other man's gut.

Murak screamed again and fell, twisting the sharp metal further into himself. MacLeod rolled away, protecting his rapidly knitting arm, hoping it was healing straight. He thought it would, but his experience with such things was only three decades old—

Murak was down, dying, but not yet defeated. He reached for MacLeod's ankle, yanked his feet out from under him as the Scot attempted to rise. His grip was a vise, biting into nerves, and MacLeod pried frantically, watching out of the corner of his eye and not entirely believing the sight of the man pulling the Arab blade out of himself, bringing his own guts with it, and lifting it over MacLeod's head.

Abandoning his effort to get loose, MacLeod lunged for the dying man's arm, forcing it up and away from him. He had heard the mad had uncanny strength, had seen strange things in battle, but this was witchcraft; he could see the light going out in the man's eyes, and still he fought. No matter that MacLeod kicked at his head, feeling the delicate facial bones shatter under his foot, no matter that the stink of his severed guts made their audience draw back; Murak fought still, and MacLeod as well, straining to keep the gleaming edge away from his head, from his neck.

And then, abruptly, it was over. Murak's eyes widened, as if in surprise, and his grip on MacLeod's ankle slackened. All the resistance went out of him, so quickly that MacLeod was unable to compensate and ended lying half on top of what was, suddenly, a dead man.

It took a moment or two for the onlookers to realize what had happened. A roar went up, as bettors on either side expressed their pleasure or dissatisfaction. MacLeod pushed himself away from the body, to his knees, and then to his feet, using the abandoned club for support. His arm was healed, but he was winded, and grateful for the crutch.

He looked up to see the captain standing on the roof of the cabin, silhouetted against the sun.

"I won," he said hoarsely. "So treat my friend."

The captain laughed. "You are an infidel. Why should I honor any promises to you?"

He stifled the urge to curse, and straightened himself. "Because half your crew are infidels too, and if you cannot keep a promise to me, why should they expect any better of you?"

The captain nodded. "A good answer, Scotsman. But it is the will of Allah that the Spaniard should die, and dead he is. See for yourself."

They cleared a path for him to the door of the cabin, and he took it, limping at first. By the time he reached his destination, the ankle was sound again. D'Alessandro and Gioninno were crouched beside d'Valenzuela, and their faces were frightened as he approached.

The body was lying still, silent.

"Is he dead?" It was impossible; it hadn't been so dreadful a wound. MacLeod himself had taken worse, before his first death. But his fellow captives nodded, and the merchant crossed himself repeatedly, muttering prayers in broken Latin.

"How?"

The captain, behind him, shrugged. "Poisoned blade, perhaps. It happens, sometimes." He waved in some of his crew. "Take this carrion and throw it overboard."

Two men moved to obey. MacLeod snarled, and the captain made another gesture; this time six men moved to subdue him.

"Chain him," the captain said, no longer interested once the immediate threat was removed. "Chain him to the mainmast. I do not think the English would pay ransom for him, but he'll do well in my lord's galleys. We'll collect a price for him."

"I am no slave!" MacLeod yelled after him, trying not to hear the sound of a splash off the port bow. "I am Duncan

MacLeod of the Clan MacLeod, and I am a slave to no man!"

The captain spared him barely a glance. "We are all the slaves of Allah. Chain him."

The winds fell almost immediately, and the captain decided to put his new captives to work at the oars. For practice, he informed them, grinning evilly.

The oarsmen were chained together at the ankles, and Gioninno, his father, and MacLeod found themselves scattered among the slaves beneath the deck. The only light came through the oarlocks.

MacLeod had not heretofore given much thought to the men below decks on the *Sancta Innocenta.* They were as motley as the crew that had conquered them—thieves, murderers, all the nationalities and races surrounding the Mediterranean and even farther north and south. The corsairs had freed the Muslim slaves immediately, but the rest they left where they were; the rowers would row, and it made no difference whether their ship flew the flag of Venice, the lilies of France, or the sword and star of Islam. MacLeod shared a bench with a former fisherman from Caesarea and a condemned man from Sardinia. They were vastly amused at the prospect of dividing their labor with one who had so recently been one of the lords above decks.

"He has soft hands," the Jew remarked to his companion, as if MacLeod were not present. "They'll be bleeding within a day."

"They will not," MacLeod retorted. "I'm no soft merchant like yon." D'Allesandro was folded over his oar, weeping, while the men on either side of him pummeled him happily.

"Oh, you're a *mercenary* then," the Sardinian said, nodding wisely. "All your calluses from a sword, I suppose. You'll find the oar less forgiving."

"I'll not be here long enough for it to forgive me."

The two laughed. "You'll be here forever, man. Or for the rest of your life," the Jew said.

"Whichever comes first," the Sardinian capped it. The two of them laughed merrily. MacLeod shuddered.

"How many men have you told that one to?"

"Three so far."

"And where are they?"

"Feeding the fishes."

"Except the Copt," the Sardinian noted.

"Ah yes, the Copt. He was sold off to Dragut Rais."

"But he's dead now too."

"Almost certainly."

The pair laughed again, slapping MacLeod on the back, wiping tears from their eyes as MacLeod looked to his right and to his left, seeing only madmen and no route of escape.

"Are you always so . . . cheerful?"

"We're slaves," the Jew said. "Of course we're cheerful. It's the greatest joke of all, don't you see?"

"No, I do not." MacLeod was beginning to feel indignant as well as dazed. He began to say something else when a command in Arabic was shouted down the deck, and his benchmates ceased their laughter and bent to their oar.

When he remained still, the two glared at him, making a show of how difficult it was to move the great oar by themselves. Shamed—it was none of their fault that they were slaves, and he was chained with them—he put his hands to the wood and helped.

"You do not seem disturbed by the Turks," he muttered. "Is it nothing to you?"

His benchmates found this exceedingly funny. "Do our chains know the religion of the men who made them?" the Jew asked. "Why should we care, as long as the ship stays above the water and not beneath it?"

"The Turks don't enslave their own," the Sardinian observed. "Which is more than one can say for the Christians. Perhaps the Muslims have more merit in the eyes of God for it."

"And my people have the greatest merit of all, then—since we don't even raid the seas."

"You ransom the ships."

"We return the innocent to their homes, and the ships to their owners."

"And all for the sake of the Turks—"

The two rowers had been over the same ground many times, it was clear. The debate was beginning to make MacLeod dizzy. "What about the woman?" he asked, grasping for the part of the discussion of most importance to him. "What about the other prisoners? Do you know what happens to them?"

"They don't come down *here*," the Sardinian snickered. "Women? They're too precious. The corsairs keep them separate for ransom—they protect them. Your woman will go to the house of the corsair until she's bought free."

"Ibn Rais," the Jew supplied helpfully. "He captured this ship last year, too. Not a bad sort. He'll feed us. You, my friend, he'll get some work out of, and then sell you in the marketplace. We'll stay here, forever and aye. Nothing changes for us."

It was all a matter of perspective, MacLeod thought. Though there was a certain amount of comfort in the thought that Terezia was not being raped and murdered as he was chained helpless below decks. He bent to his oar.

Four days later the wind came up again, and the oarsmen were given rest. By that time MacLeod was beginning to appreciate the strange and unlikely turn of humor his benchmates exhibited. When they became too annoying, he ignored them, staring past the head and shoulders of the Sardinian and out the oarlock.

He could see, now, something other than endless blue. The sky and sea were divided by a line of startling green.

"What's that?" he asked.

The Sardinian glanced out without interest. "Ah, Algiers. I hope this clan of yours has deep pockets, Scotsman. Else you'll find yourself back on a bench like this one."

"If you're lucky," the Jew added. "How many benches have such wise and witty companions, such stimulating conversation? Truly you should be grateful for such experience."

"You are both mad." But MacLeod had said that at least a dozen times in the past four days, and by now it had a certain absentminded fondness. "What is that?" They were passing a small island.

The Sardinian laughed. "Ah, the Penta. The fortress the Spanish built, to force the Moors to respect them."

"They respected them so much, they called in the Turks to level it."

"And now Sultan Abir rules in Algiers!" The Sardinian chuckled.

"The Spanish have come to regret banishing the Moors from their kingdom," the man on MacLeod's right observed. "And they regret banishing my people, too, though they'll never admit it. The music left with us."

"Spain still has music." The Scotsman was still watching the coastline, catching glimpses now of white buildings, shining in the endless, pitiless sun. "I've heard it."

"Ah, but you never heard it as it was before. The music of the fountains of Granada and Toledo was like the voices of angels."

"For a fisherman, he thinks he's a poet," the Sardinian complained. "And don't get him started on Virgil and Dante. I'll have to listen to it for months."

MacLeod grunted. He had never even learned the names of his benchmates; they had laughed at him when he had announced his own. He didn't understand how they could laugh; he didn't understand their acceptance of their fate. He felt that he ought to scorn them for accepting slavery, but something in him admired them nonetheless. Even when the whips cracked and they fell silent, bending and stretching to lift and plunge the oars into the shining waves, even when the chants went up, keeping the rhythm, they managed to trade smiles.

"Algiers . . ." The murmur ran up and down the aisle between the oarsmen's benches.

One of the corsairs came running, paused beside Gioninno, and bent to release him from the long chain running the length of the ship. The manacle remained on the boy's ankle. Yanking him up, the pirate then released and collected the merchant, and then came to MacLeod.

The three of them watched as the pirate knelt to unlock the chain, then tugged imperiously at the Scotsman's arm.

"Farewell, my friend," the Sardinian called after him. He glanced back over his shoulder to see the Jew raising his hand, pronouncing a blessing in that strange guttural language that reminded him, oddly, of home. He would never see them again.

Chapter Three

The Immortal MacLeod appears to have made friends with two of the galley slaves, but he leaves them with no signs of regret. My lord ibn Rais will sell him in the slave market of Algiers; my duty is complete. The tale of Duncan MacLeod will be taken up by another.

—Alat

Duncan MacLeod refused to acknowledge the meaning of the iron chains. He was a free man; he would not bow to an English king and before God, he would not bow to a Saracen either.

Unfortunately, the Saracens weren't interested in his opinions; he was dragged along with Gioninno and Signor d'Alessandro anyway. The *Sancta Innocenta* was docked at a long pier; he decided to wait for a better chance to escape, and spent the time trying to make sense of where he was, and perhaps even catch a glimpse of Terezia. But she was escorted from the ship in a covered palanquin, and he was disappointed.

He was well used to a variety of human beings by this time, or so he thought. Venice called herself the Queen of the Adriatic, and hosted sailors of all nations; he might have been mildly surprised by a man in tartan, but nothing else. Nothing would surprise him anymore.

Or so he thought, until he saw the turbans and robes of the people on the dock, massing to meet the *Sancta Innocenta* and other ships new come to harbor. Their clothing was all colors, white and brown and blue and yellow and green; the people themselves presented a spectrum even greater than he had seen in Venice, from pale white to darker than he could have imagined and taller than he knew a human body could grow. He stood by the rail and watched, bewildered, until the pirates pushed him onward.

The corsairs escorted their prisoners up the quay and into the mass of people and colors and noise: Algiers.

It was a white city, hurtful to the eyes in the bright sunlight. Duncan's skin had burned and healed itself so many times in the past it was nearly as dark as that of the sunburnt Arabs and Berbers who comprised most of the pirate crew, but it was still miserably hot. He couldn't imagine swathing himself in robes, as the inhabitants of this city did as a matter of course. He began to think the sun would make him as sick as the sea ever did. Then they were led into a maze of narrow passages.

Out of the direct glare, the temperature became almost bearable again, and he was able to stop squinting all the time. Behind him, Signor d'Alessandro shuffled frantically to keep up, whimpering the while. Duncan thought the corsairs must expect to make considerable money from his ransom to bother keeping him alive—but that thought reminded him of d'Valenzuela, and that in turn of the abiding fury he felt at the memory of the fight on board ship. The captain had made him fight uselessly; Alfonso was dead. So was Murak. He didn't mind killing to stay alive, or to keep someone else that way, but death for death, without even honor or glory at the end of it, was a terrible waste of human life.

Fury did nothing to melt away chains, or the manacles around his wrists and ankles and throat.

They made another turn, and found themselves at the entrance to a broad courtyard. Along one side a series of arches led to a shaded corridor within which dozens of men sat, talked, smoked, paced quietly back and forth. Toward one end a fountain played; beside it a chair was set up, almost like a throne, and upon it sat an old man with a green turban and a long white beard.

It wasn't important. Duncan scarcely saw any of it; he was looking for a more immediate threat. Somewhere in the crowd, somewhere close, he sensed another Immortal—and he was chained, weaponless, unable to defend himself.

The three prisoners were thrust out into the middle of the courtyard, and their guards wandered away, apparently abandoning them. Duncan kept turning, keeping his back to the two Italians, looking for the Immortal.

All the men in the shaded hall wore the short curved Turkish swords. Their heads were covered by turbans or kaffiyehs, and they wore ankle-length sleeveless coats over long, white gowns. Any of them could be—

MacLeod's gaze narrowed. There, sitting in the back—a small man, inoffensive looking, but watching him intently. He looked like an Arab, with his neatly trimmed brown beard. He looked as if he might be in his early forties. It meant nothing; the important thing was the sword he wore at his side, another of the short, curved Moorish blades, in a well-cared-for black leather scabbard set off with silver.

He sat on a red-and-black rug, his feet tucked up under his robe, sipping from a silver cup. His other hand rested, as if casually, on the hilt of the sword. Realizing MacLeod had identified him, he raised the cup as if in a toast, then turned back to his conversation with the man next to him as if it did not matter in the least that another of his kind had entered the courtyard, had made his city a potential battleground.

The other Immortal didn't appear inclined to approach, and anyway there were mortals present, many of them. There would be no immediate confrontation.

He wasn't afraid, only intent. For the time being he forgot why he was there, with the others; it was less important than the potential battle. His bonds were not so much a badge of shame as an impediment, one he was impatient to be rid of so that he could face the other Immortal and test himself against his opponent in honorable battle.

Impatience, however, had no place here. The three prisoners remained where they were, slowly wilting in the sun, as the men in the shade talked and sipped and moved their hands in expansive gestures, graceful salutes. The sun beat down like a hammer upon their heads, making their very hair into helmets of pain. Sweat poured off their bodies, dripped to the stone, and evaporated almost instantly. No breeze stirred the air to provide relief.

After two hours the man in the thronelike chair deigned to notice the presence of the prisoners. He leaned over and made some remark to another man sitting at his side. The other nodded, unfolded himself from the rug upon which he was sitting, and strolled out into the sunlight, over to the three of them.

He was young, wearing a long white cotton gown and a white turban, with embroidered red leather slippers that matched the curved sheath of his knife. Like all the others present, he had a beard and mustache, and there was a swagger to his step. He had to look up to meet MacLeod's eyes.

"Spanish?" he asked, in that language. His accent was fairly good.

"Scottish," MacLeod said shortly. The Moor looked puzzled. When MacLeod didn't elaborate, he shrugged and went on to the merchant and his son.

Neither of them was Spanish either. The fact that they were Italian proved of some interest, though, and the next few minutes were spent struggling to communicate. Eventually the Moor shrugged and returned to make a quiet report to the man who had sent him.

"You see," Signor d'Alessandro said to his son. He was speaking rapidly, his voice high and strained. "You see, there's nothing to be concerned about, nothing, they'll send a message, we'll be ransomed. Soon. Soon. They'll treat us well. We'll find your sister, too."

As far as MacLeod could see, no one was interested in how well or badly they were treated. Gioninno didn't seem interested either; his face was pale, his thin chest dark red from the sun, and he was sweating copiously. MacLeod could sympathize. He was feeling rather lightheaded himself.

Now another man came from the shade into the sunlight to look them over, as they themselves might have looked over horses at a fair. MacLeod wondered whether he might not even insist on looking at their teeth. He even raised his hand to probe at the long muscles of MacLeod's arm, until he caught the expression in his eyes and thought better of it.

Yet another came to consider them more closely—this time their interviewer wore a long black coat, with long curls of hair over his ears.

Gioninno staggered. The new inspector lost interest.

No one else came. After a while their captors came back, took their chains, and led them out of the courtyard and back into the blessed shade of the maze of corridors made by the many-storied walls of the houses of Algiers. Gioninno actually cried out with relief. MacLeod couldn't blame him; the drop in temperature was a shock to his system, too. Signor d'Alessandro was too busy talking to notice.

The corridors were like warrens, stone paths between white walls interrupted at intervals by doors a little taller than MacLeod was. The doors appeared identical but must have had something to distinguish them, as their escort showed no uncertainty when they dragged their prisoners to a stop. One of the pirates beat upon the cracked wood, and the door opened, and the three prisoners were herded inside. They stumbled along a short passageway and then, startlingly, outside again.

Behind the featureless walls lay a courtyard: a garden, with a fountain, surrounded by a shaded arched passage. Above it was a similar balcony, surmounted by yet another. Stairways in the corners led from one floor to another.

They barely noticed. The sun was setting; the fountain, the beautiful, dancing water, was in shade, and they didn't even have to brave the sunlight to get to it, to throw themselves half into it and lave the burns and sweat from their bodies. It was close to the most wonderful sensation any of them had ever experienced.

"Upstairs," one of the pirates said, when he felt the captives had had enough. When they ignored him, he grabbed them by their hair and forcibly pulled them out of the water, snatched the wet chains, and pulled them along.

"Food," he explained when they made as if to resist. As he spoke, he slid the chains out of the loops on their wrists and ankles, freeing them from each other at last.

It was enough to get their cooperation. MacLeod had never thought mere stairs would be too much for him, but it was a long flight, and steep—

—and at the top, Paradise: a large room with cots arranged around the perimeter, and a table heaped with plates of grapes and dates and figs and bread, a tall silver coffeepot surrounded by tiny cups. The three captives fell upon the food like starving wolves, scarcely noticing when the door drew shut behind them with a decisive *click*.

There was no meat, but it would have spoiled too quickly in the heat anyway. After the first few bolted mouthfuls, Duncan slowed and took the time to look around as he ate.

The coffeepot puzzled him. He had tasted coffee before, in Italy, and disliked it. He knew it was a common drink in the Turkish lands. But silver? For captives?

The coffeepot was an elegant thing, tall and spare, with a long, narrow, delicately curved spout and a handle with a matching arch. The cups were lined with impossibly thin glass. The metal was plain, not etched with any design, but still would not shame the table of many a European nobleman, assuming they drank such stuff.

Neither d'Alessandro nor his son bothered with it. MacLeod picked up the vessel and looked it over thoughtfully, appreciating it. Perhaps their captor was wealthier than he'd looked. He replaced it on the table and continued looking about.

There were three windows, each blocked by a latticework of wooden strips painted white, too small for a man to crawl through—and besides, they overlooked the interior courtyard. And even if he managed to get out of the house, he was still in Algiers, a strange city, a strange land, inhabited by strange people with customs and a language he didn't know.

Before he had died for the first time—before he had awakened from that death—he had had no time for foreign ways. Afterward, driven out of his clan territory by his own kin— by those he had always considered his own kin—he had lived by his sword, literally as well as figuratively. But in so doing he had discovered there was more to the world than the Highlands, even though he still ached for them.

It was too soon to go home; it had only been thirty years. There were still those who might remember Duncan

MacLeod of the Clan MacLeod as one of those accursed ones—like the man rumored in his grandfather's time, who was killed in battle and did not stay decently dead. The man he had called "Father" had repudiated him to his face, telling him he was a foundling, and not a MacLeod, in truth, at all.

He had claimed the name and the clan anyway, and sworn never to give it up. He bit into a sweet date and smiled to himself. None of his fellow clansmen would know what to do with themselves here either. There was no shame in ignorance, only in remaining in that state. None of his fellow clansmen could read and write, either, but he and Fitzcairn had learned how; if he could do that, he could learn the ways of Algiers.

His gaze fell upon the manacle about his wrist, and his lips tightened. He'd forgotten them, momentarily; his body was getting used to them, as to bracelets of finer metal.

He wouldn't be a slave. Not to the English, not to the Turks, not to anyone.

That was an issue he would settle later. Just now, he was only a prisoner. He could accept defeat in honorable battle; defeats were temporary things.

As long as it was honorable. The image of d'Valenzuela haunted him. MacLeod had risked his life, and the man had died anyway. And yet, mad as it seemed, it had been worthwhile; it was the principle of the thing that counted.

He reached for a piece of bread, but his hand fell to his side before he touched it. He was very tired, suddenly. Looking around, he saw the merchant and his son collapsed on two of the thick mats. D'Alessandro was snoring, open-mouthed. His son, a thinner version of himself, was doing the same.

Another mat, against the opposite wall, waited for him. It was thick with piled fleeces smelling faintly of sheep grease,

and woven rugs in dyes of red and blue and green and yellow
and black.

The rugs were unfamiliar, but the fleeces were not. Before
he knew it, he was burying his face in them, and dreaming of
a place where it was cool, and there were mountains, and
greenery, and mists in the morning.

Chapter Four

═══

*It will be necessary to follow the Scottish Immortal
through the slave market. It is unlikely that the Sultan
will buy him on the third day, as another had already
expressed interest. We may soon bring the Chronicle
of Duncan MacLeod to a close; I will inquire whether
it will be necessary to add him to my duties, which
are already considerable.*

         —Thierry Estevan

The three prisoners were awakened the next morning, early,
by a strange, musical wail that echoed from the roofs of the
city. MacLeod was awakened from a dream of an Italian
summer's day to find it was still dark outside, the sky barely
lightening. The call came again, and again, and the stillness
of night began to shift, and whisper, and rouse itself. The call
came again, and again, echoing. The memory of where he
was, and under what conditions, returned to him.

He rose to his feet, silently, and moved across the room to
the latticed window. Through it he watched the courtyard
below gradually take on substance with the light, watched a
half-dozen of the corsairs file quietly in, each carrying something rolled up under an arm.

Rugs: they were rugs, small ones. The men lined up, facing the wall that hid from them the rising sun, and laid the rugs out in a neat line. And then they stood, and knelt, and crouched down in abasement, murmuring all the while as the sky brightened, repeating the process twice more. Then, the morning prayer finished, the men rose, picked up their rugs, and filed out again, leaving the courtyard empty save for the doves, cooing and preening on the rim of the fountain.

"What were they doing?" It was Gioninno, standing at his elbow. He was speaking very quietly, as if afraid he might wake his father.

Duncan looked at him with something akin to pity. The boy was shivering, even in the heat of the morning. His thin chest was pale and quivering—he had looked much older in silks and satins and jewels. He had even looked older with that ridiculous toy sword in his hand, threatening pirates like a lady's lap dog. Now he only looked like a scared boy, looking for reassurance.

"Praying. They were praying."

"It wasn't a church. How do you know?" It was the kind of challenge that came from fear; Duncan had seen it before. He'd even made it himself, a time or two.

"I saw slaves pray in Italy so."

"They're heathens." Gioninno peered down into the empty courtyard, as if he could still see them, rising and bowing and pressing their heads against the stone. "They'll burn for eternity, all of them."

Duncan quirked his eyebrows and made no response. He was a fighter, not a philosopher, and certainly not a churchman. He was less concerned about his immortal soul than he used to be; as long as it remained within his immortal body, he was satisfied. He could afford to be complacent about heathens.

"What are they going to do to us?" Gioninno's voice quavered. "What about Terezia? Are we really going to be ransomed? Father says so, but—"

"Aye, you probably will, soon enough." Of course, it would take months for the message to go back to Venice and the money to be raised and returned, and all that against the chance that the messenger might be wrecked or captured as well; but there was no point in frightening the boy further.

"But what about you? Do you have anyone?"

Duncan smiled slightly, imagining the reaction of the Clan MacLeod to the news that the carrier of the family curse was being held by the Turks and would like to dip into the family coffers to be bought free, please. Or maybe Fitzcairn would have a little silver put by—unless he'd seen a pretty girl to spend it on.

"They'll make you a slave, won't they?"

MacLeod glanced down at the manacles about his wrists. "I'm no slave." He had no idea where Fitz was, anyway.

"MacLeod . . ."

The boy was going to tell him he was scared, MacLeod could tell. He didn't want to hear it; he particularly didn't want the boy to say it. Once said, it couldn't be unsaid.

"Where's the chamber pot?" he asked hastily. "And is there any food left?"

Across the room, Signor d'Alessandro stirred and groaned.

"Do you suppose they'll come for us soon?" Gioninno asked plaintively. "Or will they leave us here?"

"I doubt they'll leave us." The chamberpot was tucked conveniently away in a corner.

Minutes later, as Duncan picked his way disappointedly through the remains of the food on the table, d'Alessandro lunged into wakefulness. It took him somewhat longer to remember where he was, and required a reminder from his son. While they talked, Duncan grimaced, seized the last date, and ate it, wondering what it would take to get a decent plate of mutton stew in Algiers. He was still occupied with the thought, and trying to ignore the merchant's wails, when the door opened and several of the corsairs entered, carrying chains.

"Och, no," he said.

The corsairs didn't speak English, but they didn't need to in order to understand the look on his face. They glanced at each other nervously, shoving each other forward. Duncan grinned without humor. "Which of you little men wants to try to put those back on me?"

D'Alessandro moaned in terror. One of the pirates, recognizing easier prey, edged along the wall toward the merchant and his son.

"I don't think you ought to put them back on my friends, either," MacLeod said, stepping toward the man.

D'Alessandro broke into a babble of disclaimers, the gist of which was that neither he nor his son knew this madman, that he and his son were happy to cooperate, if only the Signores Corsaires would refrain from drawing their swords, the finest products of Damascus they were, surely—

"Ah, that's done it," MacLeod observed with disgust, as the corsairs, reminded of the steel they wore, drew the weapons and held them menacingly as they advanced once more on MacLeod. "You could not manage to keep your mouth shut just one moment longer?"

D'Alessandro was helping the Turk thread the chains through the loops on his wrist manacles. Giving him a disgusted look, MacLeod executed a strategic retreat to the mats on the floor, snatched up a sheepskin, and wrapped it around his arm as a shield. It made a massive, bulky roll.

Somehow the leader of the expedition wasn't properly impressed with his protection. The man gave Duncan a gap-toothed grin, and the sword sliced down.

A thick fleece, and a well-tanned hide, wrapped in layers, wouldn't have deflected a blow from a good Scottish broadsword, but it would have blunted it. If a man his own size had delivered it, he would expect perhaps a broken arm.

He did not, however, expect to feel steel slicing through all the layers and deep into the muscles of his arm. A shock of white pain hit him and then, almost immediately, began to recede as the hidden injury began to heal. The corsair, who had felt steel hit bone, grinned at the look that crossed MacLeod's face and swung the sword again, only as a threat this time, and held out a fistful of chains. The alternative he was offering was clear.

MacLeod backed away, holding the wrapped arm before him, hoping it hadn't bled too badly before closing. His opponent, still expecting him to fall over or at least scream, began to look aggrieved, and swung again. This time Duncan stepped out of the sword's path. There was no point, after all, in either making the man more suspicious or in suffering another wound, rapidly healing or not.

Unfortunately, the other pirates, having shuffled the chained Italians out of the room, could now turn their attentions to Duncan as well, and there wasn't enough room to avoid them all. He eyed them warily, trying to maneuver them into each other's way, hoping somehow to disarm one and acquire one of the lethally sharp curved swords for himself. He had to be armed; he couldn't escape from this place without some means to defend himself from the other Immortal he had discovered in the courtyard—

It was too late. He could feel that other presence now, somewhere near. Somewhere in the house— MacLeod shouted and lunged at the nearest pirate, hoping to take him by surprise, ducking inside his guard to grab his wrist. It would have worked, too, if it hadn't been for the pile of fleeces scattered from the sleeping mats. He bore his target down to the floor, but was unable to get purchase before the others were upon him. He looked up from the floor to find five Saracen blades hovering at his throat, and past them to see the Immortal from the day before, standing in the doorway and watching him with a quizzical look on his face. He was dressed in the by-now familiar white gown the others wore, and the open, brown sleeveless coat; his hair was covered by the same white turban he had worn the day before.

"You are not very old, are you?" the Immortal said, in beautifully accented Spanish.

"I am Duncan MacLeod of the Clan MacLeod," he spat in the same language, trying to get to his feet. The swords pressed in on him. "I'll meet you in honorable battle . . ."

The other Immortal raised one elegant hand. "Peace be upon you, Duncan MacLeod. I am Hamza ibn Mohammed al Katib, sometimes honored by the name el Kahir, and I have no wish to take your head."

The corsairs, confused by this exchange, were sneaking glances over their shoulders at Hamza and then back at MacLeod. Hamza spoke to them in Arabic, and their leader answered him. After some discussion, the swords withdrew, disappearing into sheaths, and they gave MacLeod room to get to his feet. The pirate he had pinned beneath him gasped something obscene and crawled away, glaring.

"I have told them you will be coming with me," Hamza informed him cheerfully.

"Why?" MacLeod was still suspicious.

"Because I have purchased you from our gracious Sultan, upon his head be peace. Also, it allows you to avoid going to the slave market once again."

"I'll wear no chains."

"I have assured them no chains will be required. Our law says you must have the manacle about one ankle, however, unless you wish to profess Islam, in which case you will be freed."

"I am no heathen!"

"No," Hamza said composedly, "you are an infidel. But God is compassionate."

Unable to argue with that, at least, MacLeod shrugged. Then another thought occurred to him. "What about Gioninno and his father?" Unwrapping the fleece from his arm, he folded it as he did so to hide the massive bloodstain from the still-angry corsairs. "Have you—purchased—them too?"

Hamza laughed. "I am not so wealthy a man. Besides, they have welcomed their chains; who am I to deprive them of the opportunity of wearing them?"

Duncan paused at that, and looked at him more closely. It was true; d'Alessandro had been eager to submit, to avoid a battle. "Gioninno deserves better," he said. "He followed his father's lead."

"As it is appropriate for a son to do. They are not my concern. You are, Duncan MacLeod."

"I am not a slave," he repeated. It was a warning, and an article of faith.

"We are all the slaves of God. Come with me, Duncan MacLeod. Get dressed, please, and let us see what you make of the city of Algiers."

Chapter Five

*However unlikely it may seem, Hamza el Kahir
appears to have taken Duncan MacLeod under his
tutelage. It is most disconcerting, as the Scotsman is
an uncouth, unlettered, uncivilized barbarian. The
ways of Immortals are truly mysterious.*

—Estevan

It was not, perhaps, so much what Duncan MacLeod made of
the city of Algiers, as what the city made of him. He was
head and shoulders taller than most of the natives, and even
dressed in the long white gown and the headcloth he was
still, unmistakably, European. His unfamiliarity and discom-
fort with the length of the thobe—it felt as if it would tangle
around his ankles—made it even more obvious. He could
feel the stares following him, even as he followed Hamza
through the city of Algiers. At least he had a robe to cover
himself, and something on his head, and sandals. But no
sword.

He was still not quite sure that the Moor hadn't purchased
him only to take his head. But the corsairs clearly respected
the man, and even when they were left alone he made no

threat. Duncan decided, cautiously, that perhaps he could be trusted.

Hamza led him through the maze of shaded alleys again, and then along wider streets. Glancing along the crossways, Duncan could catch glimpses of movement, veils of dust and color and noise. "What's that?"

"Ah, the marketplace. We can visit it, perhaps."

"Can I get a sword there?" Duncan asked bluntly. "I have to be able to defend myself."

Hamza nodded. "That is very true. The swords you will find here are of poor quality, I fear, but even the worst of them are very different from your English broadswords."

"Scottish," MacLeod corrected sharply.

"As you say." Hamza nodded graciously. "Here. Welcome to my house, Duncan MacLeod. Enter and be at peace."

He was standing at one of the featureless doors in the wall, his hand laid upon it. He did not, as far as the Scotsman could see, knock upon it or make any signal. Nonetheless, the door opened, and Hamza led him within the walls, through a narrow hallway, and out the other end into the inevitable courtyard and garden.

The place was filled with the perfume of things growing and blooming, beautiful living things. The falling water of a fountain made sweet music, and a pair of orange trees provided shade and scent. For all the heat of the day, the touch of water in the air was like a cool caress against his skin.

"It's like a piece of Paradise," he blurted out, and then, "I mean—I don't intend to blaspheme—"

"I am not offended," Hamza said. "Though this can only be the most faded shadow of Paradise. Remain here awhile, Highlander. It is not, perhaps, holy ground, but I swear by my head you are safe in this place."

"By your—" It was an oath an Immortal could not make

lightly. Hamza's brown eyes were serious as he waited to see how his guest would react.

Duncan nodded finally. "Very well."

There were rules to life in a Moorish home, MacLeod found out over the next few weeks. He could use only his right hand to eat; he was made to wash incessantly; when he stretched out his legs Hamza slashed at the exposed soles of his feet for the disrespect they showed.

It was a matter of adopting the customs of the land, Hamza explained, when he objected, sometimes loudly. If he was to live a long time, he needed to know how to blend in. Showing the soles of his feet to his host in an Arab land would emphatically not make him blend in.

He conceded, grumpily, that Hamza was right; anyway, the riding crop hadn't actually hurt. Much.

After a while he stopped spinning vain plots to escape and realized that he was being given an opportunity to learn a whole new culture. Algiers might be closer to Scotland than Venice, but only in the geographic sense. And it was the most religious place he'd ever seen; not even excepting the Kirk back home. The household prayed five times a day, starting with Hamza himself, and including everyone, even the women.

That was another thing he could barely understand. He rarely saw the women, and there were too many of them.

"*How* many wives?" he sputtered one day, as they ate a light lunch of dates and figs and bread in the little courtyard of Hamza's home. He had lived in Hamza's home for three months, and thought of himself now as a student rather than a slave.

"Only three," Hamza said, smiling. "I cannot afford a fourth and maintain them all as the Prophet commands. Have you never been married, MacLeod?"

MacLeod flinched. It was still a painful subject, even after so long; the memory of Debra Campbell and Robert MacLeod would haunt him for a long time. He had loved Debra, truly loved her, and she had been betrothed to his cousin. And both of them had died, and he felt guilty of both their deaths, even after so long. He shook himself and made himself answer facetiously. "Not even once! And I think it's damned greedy of you!"

Hamza laughed. "I am not responsible for your shortcomings, Scotsman. Or your lack of ambition."

"But you canna have bairns—"

The confusion on Hamza's face made MacLeod start over in Spanish. His Arabic was getting better, slowly; Hamza's English was improving as well, but he spoke with an odd accent, adopting some of MacLeod's burr. When they wanted to communicate easily, their common ground was Spanish.

"You can't have children—can you?"

A shadow crossed Hamza's face. "It is the will of God that such as we, who have His blessing in so many ways, should not have this as well. God is most great."

"Er, aye." MacLeod fell silent. He wasn't sure how to respond; the Muslim references to the will of God struck him as fatalism. While he had somewhat of an affinity for that particular mindset himself, his own inclination was to take action, any action. Resignation wasn't part of his makeup.

"Let us go to the camel market, and the coffee house, and see what the day brings." Hamza smiled. "Ibn Rais has received the ransom, at least for the men captured with you. But there was no one to pay your price, so he has given me a gift of gold to make up for my loss. He is most generous."

"As are you, my friend." The mention of the ransom raised another issue, one which had never been far from MacLeod's mind. He looked down at his plate and pushed a date back and forth with a fingertip. "You know I am grateful for all you have done for me, Hamza."

"It has been my great pleasure to have you as my guest," the other man responded. His brows were slightly knit, as if waiting for what was coming.

"What of Terezia?" MacLeod continued softly. "I haven't forgotten her, you know. The men were ransomed; if she was not, this time—I cannot let her remain with ibn Rais. It has been far too long already." He closed his eyes for a moment, remembering his last sight of her, descending below deck, depending on him to protect her. While events were in train for her to be ransomed, he could comfort himself that nothing would harm her—in the market for captives as all else, damaged goods were worth less. But now he was no longer certain.

Hamza looked puzzled. "Why can you not leave her where she is? I have told you many times. He has no doubt used her kindly; the price he asked was too high, perhaps, for them to pay all at once. It is not unknown for such things to happen. If her family pays in a little while it will be well; she will return home. If her family does not pay it will be well also; she will convert, and he will marry her. It is how these things are done. And my friend, it has only been three months."

Duncan's hand tightened on the piece of bread he was eating, and he set it aside. "Hamza, I cannot. She is a woman. I have a duty to protect her. I cannot leave her with him. Until now, I have not known enough to be able to get about. Now I think perhaps I could. I have to do *something*, Hamza."

Hamza settled on the other side of the round table, tucking his feet carefully beneath his robe, and reached for a cluster of grapes. "From what are you protecting her?" he inquired. He bit one of the globes in half, scooped out the seeds, and ate the rest with evident enjoyment. "In either case she will be safe, and married."

Duncan opened his mouth to explain that most Europeans

had a jaundiced view of the fate of women who remained unredeemed in the hands of Algerian pirates, and decided against it. "It is a matter of honor, Hamza. The man who was sworn to protect her was my friend. He died on board the *Sancta Innocenta*. And if her father and brother have been ransomed, she is truly all alone."

"Ah. Honor. That explains it, then." Hamza ate another grape. "You are not, of course, interested in the woman yourself."

Despite himself, MacLeod grinned ruefully. "Perhaps a little."

"Perhaps you will be the one to marry her, and be less concerned about other men's greed?"

Duncan shook his head. "Och, no. I'm far from ready to marry!" *Not with Debra gone . . .* "But she's a good girl. She belongs in her own home, with her family."

"And how will you get her there? And will they not reject her in any case, since her virtue is already in question?" There was a certain wryness in Hamza's tone.

Duncan, who was ready to leap to his feet and effect a rescue, stopped. "Ah. I assumed you would help me."

Hamza shook his head, smiling. "Duncan MacLeod, ibn Rais is my friend. And I am a poor man and can purchase neither the girl nor passage to an infidel port. She is not one of us. Forget her."

"I canna."

"Then as I said. Let us go to the camel market, and the coffee house, and see what the day brings. Perhaps some thought will occur to us."

"Don't see how you can think anything at all in the heat of that sun," Duncan muttered, following.

The camel market of Algiers, quite frankly, stank.

Just outside the desert-side city walls, it was a mass of

tents and people and animals: black tents, tents striped black and brown and dingy white; veiled Taureg men whose skin, where it showed, appeared to be dyed blue, walking fierce and free and arrogant as any man from the Highlands; merchants and tribesmen and sailors; shouting men on small quick horses of grey and bay and black. There were flies everywhere, large black buzzing ones massing over piles of manure.

And the camels. Loud bawling nasty beasties they were, some of them resting on folded legs, some standing, near twice as tall as many men; all of them looking at him haughtily under lowered lids and long, long eyelashes. They were haltered and tied to stakes or long lines. Hamza was engaged almost immediately in animated discussion with one of the camel dealers regarding one of his charges. Duncan looked at the beast and could not for the life of him understand why anyone would want such a poor misshapen thing—humpbacked, they were, and with great knobby knees and ridiculous tails, and heads swimming back and forth on long thin stalky necks.

The camel looked him in the eye, opened its mouth, and bawled deafeningly, sending MacLeod staggering back several steps. This turned out to be a very good thing, because the animal then proceeded to work its long, flexible lips as if about to laugh, and then it spit at him.

Duncan looked aghast at the wad of green spittle sliding down the front of his robe.

"Here now!" he shouted at the animal. "How dare you!"

The camel regarded him with sublime disdain and yawned, revealing incredibly long, yellow teeth in its lower jaw. Duncan took one step closer to the animal, clutching at his belt for a nonexistent hilt.

The camel's head snaked forward, and the animal snapped at him. He dodged back, cursing, and stepped into a pile of camel leavings to the sound of laughter from the watching camel dealer and Hamza.

The camel hadn't even bothered to lurch to its feet.

Duncan looked from the camel to his audience to the mess on his leather shoes. He had no weapon—slaves were not permitted such things, after all—and the animal had insulted him—

With great deliberation, he worked up a mouthful of saliva and spat back, hitting the camel directly on the nose.

The camel yelled, rose in a three-part jerk to its feet, and staggered as far away as its tether would permit. Duncan gave a satisfied nod, scraped his shoe as clean as he could get it, and swaggered over to Hamza and the dealer. "That'll teach him," he announced.

Hamza and the dealer howled with laughter and slapped him on the back. "Someone should tell the Vizier," the dealer gasped. "The infidels have a secret weapon."

"Indeed," Hamza responded, wiping a tear from his eye. "They will rise up and spit at the Mamluks—"

"Aye, but it's only Scottish spit that has the virtue," Duncan said, eyes dancing. "Ye'll have nothing to worry about from the Spanish. They canna handle the whisky."

Still laughing, Hamza led Duncan away. "It was a very poor excuse for a she-camel anyway," he consoled him. "He usually sells pack animals. That one is too light."

Duncan looked back at the camel, now tearing busily into a pile of hay. It looked substantial enough to him.

"I'll take your word for it," he muttered.

They threaded their way through another dealer's animals, and waited as a caravan passed.

"Y'have the strangest animals," Duncan said thoughtfully, watching the camels swaying by, the loads on their backs piled into high V-shaped frames. Trotting at their sides were the occasional young one and the caravan guards, most riding the small horses with the large eyes and light step. Duncan had heard they ran like the wind. They were bred by the tribes of the vast Sahara. The contract they made with the Roman-nosed beasts was startling, especially when one cantered by the other. "Those little things. How can they bear the weight of a grown man?"

"They're stronger than they look," Hamza remarked idly. He glanced up at the sun. "It is nearly time for the afternoon prayer. Come with me."

Turning his back on the caravan, he led Duncan down an alley and around too many corners to count, until they came to a square dominated by another plain white building with a tall tower at one corner. Outside the door to the building were rows upon rows of shoes.

Hamza removed his own shoes and added them to a row, indicating to Duncan to do likewise.

"Why are we—" Duncan started to ask.

"This is holy ground," Hamza informed him. "Enter, and remain at the back, and wait for me."

Duncan was still getting used to the fact that a mosque qualified as holy ground. This was not a church; it wasn't even a shrine to one of those ancient, nearly forgotten gods one found from time to time in Europe. This was heathen, Muslim.

He watched Hamza join the lines of men unrolling prayer rugs as the call of the muezzin rang out over the white walls of Algiers. It was answered by another call from another quarter, and another, until for one moment he felt as if he could step upon the threads of sound and climb up to the blue and white mosaic ceiling of the mosque.

The rows of men stood, and knelt, and bowed down, touching their foreheads to the floor in obeisance, saying the proper words with each movement; and stood, and knelt, and bowed again, and again, praying in unison, in wholehearted submission to the will of Allah. Duncan watched Hamza among them, listened to the prayers, and thought about it.

Then he shrugged. Holy ground was holy ground. He was not a follower of Diana, either, and he respected her sacred groves; well enough, then. This too was a safe place in the endless battle of Immortal against Immortal. He could honor that.

The prayer was ended. Hamza bent down and rolled up his prayer rug, placing it against the wall, and returned to collect Duncan. They went outside again and joined the crowd of men putting their shoes back on.

"Five times a day?" Duncan inquired. "Every day?"

"So the Koran commands us."

"I see." Duncan tried to remember the last time he had attended church regularly, and winced.

Hamza exchanged greetings with some of the other men, brushing off their hostile glances at the alien in their midst, and he and Duncan continued on their way.

"Why were you talking to the camel dealer, anyway? Is it a hobby with you? I knew a MacDonald like that. Poor as a church mouse, he was, but he couldna stay away from a horse fair. . . ." Duncan was babbling, still disconcerted by the thought of Muslim holy ground.

"I thought you were intent upon rescuing the Lady Terezia," Hamza said.

"I am. What has that to do with camels?"

"But it is as I told you, Duncan MacLeod: I cannot hire a ship. I am a poor man. But I can rent a camel."

Duncan blinked, looked at the other man, and smiled.

Chapter Six

Hamza and the Scottish Immortal seem to have established a firm friendship. If the foreigner remains in Algiers, I will be assigned to Watch him permanently.

—Tezanaya el'Amin

"This is the house of Abdul Mohammed ibn Rais," Hamza said, waving a casual hand at yet one more blank white wall. It was two days later, and they were walking through the maze of narrow passages that passed for streets in the residential quarter of the city.

"How can you tell?" Duncan asked, giving the wall a narrow glare. "It looks like every other wall in Algiers. It must be hell getting home when you're drunk."

Hamza's eyebrows climbed. "Spirituous liquors are forbidden to us," he said, with a touch of annoyance.

"Your Prophet was looking after your interests," Duncan said, looking up and down the narrow alley at the featureless walls. The wall stretched up six feet over their heads. There were no doors to break the expanse, from which Duncan deduced that this must be a back wall.

"Do not mock the Prophet," Hamza said, very softly. He

fingered the rough-hammered hilt of the sword he always wore.

Duncan abruptly realized two things: one, that he still wore no sword of his own, and two, that once again he had crossed an invisible line with the other man. He decided the better part of valor was to go scuttling back across it. "I wasna mocking him. It's but the truth!"

Hamza's expression softened minutely, and Duncan followed up on the advantage. "Is this the place his corsairs took us? It doesna look familiar. Though God knows how I could tell."

"God is merciful and compassionate, even to the Scots," Hamza sighed.

"Have you mentioned that to the Sassenach lately?" Duncan fumbled for the word, unable to find it in Spanish and reduced to using Gaelic instead.

Hamza was confused. "The who?"

"Sassenach. You know, the spawn of the devil— Oh, never mind." Duncan placed the flat of his hand against the wall. "You didna answer me."

"What—ah yes. It is as I said: ibn Rais is a friend of mine. This is indeed the place you were taken. It is his home—"

"So you're going to help me break into your friend's home and steal away Terezia?"

Hamza's eyebrows arched again. "Help you? You're mad. I am merely pointing out the sights of Algiers."

"For example, observe the crenellation opposite." Hamza jutted his chin at a projection in the wall across the alley. "Often, often we have told ibn Rais that verily, it is an invitation to the Evil One, who inspires his followers to throw ropes—"

"I'm Scottish. I don't need advice from the Evil One, thank you."

Hamza shrugged.

Duncan studied the situation further. "And what might be behind this wall?"

"I do not know. I would conjecture that it is the women's quarters."

"And why would you conjecture that?"

Hamza shrugged again. "Because that is where I keep the women of my own household. One does not wish to have them in the forefront of the house, after all."

Duncan, remembering his own mother—foster mother, he reminded himself with a stab of the old hurt, recalling his banishment—could only shake his head at the thought that anyone could tuck her away in the back of the house. Mary MacLeod took second place to no man. She would not have gotten on well in Algiers at all.

Lady Terezia, as spritely and intelligent and beautiful as she was, had not quite the same strength of character, in his estimation. Still, she was probably bearing up well, or so he hoped.

"How do I know your friend ibn Rais hasn't already, er, had his way with Terezia?" he fretted yet again.

"Ibn Rais is no fool," Hamza said patiently, for what seemed the thousandth time. "He would not devalue the merchandise. He wishes to sell her back to her family, after all."

"I don't think her family will believe it."

"They can always have her examined. She will not be the first woman taken by our shipmen."

Duncan winced.

"Besides, if she was to marry a Spaniard, her intended might be related to one of our own families. That being so, he might be most respectful of her. It is not so very long since they drove us out of Granada."

Duncan glanced at him sharply, to see if he were being teased, but Hamza's voice had a distinct tinge of nostalgia. It was a reference to the Moorish city in Spain, a place of gardens and fountains, of culture and science, where the Moors and the Jews and the Christians had lived together amicably until Isabella of Castile and her husband of Aragon had fulfilled their oath to banish all but Catholics from their joint kingdom.

Not so very long? It had been a hundred and forty years earlier, and a piece of history Duncan had heard of only in passing. It hadn't seemed very important at the time.

It was, obviously, important to Hamza. It was no wonder he spoke such flawless Spanish. MacLeod experienced a sudden chill. It had been only thirty years since he himself had "died" . . . but to remember a city from a hundred and forty years ago . . . He was beginning to realize what it truly meant to be Immortal. He wondered, suddenly, if he too would one day live to remember something that had happened four or five lifetimes ago. He had "died" and lived again often enough to believe in what he was—but he was still learning all that it meant, and sometimes it still frightened him.

And he didn't know how old Hamza actually was. He might have seen the Prophet he revered so with his own eyes. He might even have seen the Christian prophet, whom the Muslims honored second only to Mohammed. He crossed himself at the thought.

Hamza was watching him as if he knew exactly what MacLeod was thinking, as if he had had such thoughts himself, centuries ago. But his next words had nothing to do with history.

"It is illegal for slaves to bear weapons," he said in a businesslike tone. "But suicide is unseemly, and for one of us to go unarmed is even more so. We must correct this matter."

"Aye. Although I wouldna mind a look at yon wee sword as cut through a good fleece as if it werena there—"

"What?" There were times when MacLeod's brogue made even his Spanish nearly unintelligible.

"Your scimitars. Are they all so sharp? They'd break if they hit aught solid, but—"

"Like this one?" Grinning evilly, Hamza whipped his silver-hilted sword out of its curved sheath. MacLeod backed away, gaze darting back and forth looking desperately for something in the empty alley to use to defend himself. He didn't really believe Hamza wanted his head, but there were no mortals around to stop them, and it was not holy ground—

Hamza chuckled and put the weapon away. "It would not break if it hit your neck, infidel, I assure you. Come with me, and I will show you the finest swords in Algiers—none of which I can afford—and we will have coffee, and talk of your visit to the house of my good friend ibn Rais, and what you are likely to find there."

"I still don't really understand why you're helping me against your friend now, when you wouldn't before," MacLeod muttered abstractedly. "I'm grateful, mind. I just don't understand."

Hamza, for reasons of his own, chose to ignore him.

Most of MacLeod's attention was focused, anyway, on the row upon row of steel blades lined up before him. They were all curved. Most had the shimmer of Damascus steel, catching the light of the early-afternoon sun and casting it back again in rainbows. A few of the swords were etched and inscribed, like Hamza's. The hilts ranged from plain wood to inlaid ivory and turquoise and jewels.

MacLeod was more interested in their edges than their decorations. While Hamza engaged the merchant in conversation, he ran a thumb curiously along one glittering edge.

He couldn't even feel the skin part. He didn't realize he

had been cut, or how deeply, until he saw the blood well up and saw his own flesh overlapping the steel. Then the pain came, a sharp cold jab that made his nerves shudder even as he snatched back his hand, watched with a curiosity not yet jaded as the split thumb came back together and healed, leaving only the blood to mark the injury.

"You are not used to a decent blade," the swordseller remarked, cleaning the smear from the metal. He lifted the sword out of the rack and hefted it, showing off its balance.

"It's sharp enough," MacLeod allowed, surreptitiously wiping his thumb clean. "But a blade that sharp has no strength to it."

"Do you think so?" the merchant said. "Now, by God, I think you should try it. Look you." From a pile of odds and ends stacked untidily just inside the open wing of his tent, he drew out a silk scarf, a sheer billow of white floating in the wind. The material was nearly transparent in its fineness. "What would happen if you cut at this with one of your great European swords?"

Duncan shrugged.

"And this." The swordsweller produced an iron bar, perhaps two fingers thick.

Duncan grinned. "Aye, that we could handle well enough."

The merchant started to hand the sword to him, then hesitated. "Hamza?" he said. "Perhaps it is better so—" With that he held it out to the other Moor.

Hamza smiled apologetically at MacLeod. "It is the law," he explained. "It would be madness to provide weapons to captives, after all."

Duncan stifled his disappointment and watched as the other Immortal swung the sword experimentally. "Not one of your better blades," he informed the merchant critically.

"The eye of Hamza el Kahir is unequalled," the merchant

acknowledged. "Truly it is a lesser blade." He snapped his wrist, and the silk scarf spread out and floated gently downward.

In a move not even MacLeod's eye could follow, Hamza's arm snapped out, and suddenly there were two scarves, not one, floating nearly undisturbed to the earth.

MacLeod blinked, and his eyes widened. "Holy Mother of God, is that a sword or a razor?"

"He blasphemes!" the merchant snapped.

"He is an infidel," Hamza answered. "Now, the rod, I think."

Distracted from his outrage by the opportunity to have his wares tested by what was clearly a recognized master, the merchant made his way out from behind the rack of swords and the display table and stood in the little passageway. Other merchants and customers stopped what they were doing to watch as the merchant stood, feet braced, and raised the bar horizontally over his head, holding it at either end.

"Ah, no," MacLeod started to object. "It's a bonny little blade, there's no need to ruin it—"

It was too late. Hamza's arm went back and over and down, and with a painfully sharp clang the sword connected with the iron bar. Sparks flew.

And the merchant staggered, holding now a shorter bar in either hand.

The watching audience laughed and made approving noises.

MacLeod's eyes went wider still, and he moved up to Hamza's shoulder, looking over it at the scimitar, now undergoing intense scrutiny from the Immortal.

"Tch," Hamza said disapprovingly, pointing to a nearly invisible nick in the edge of the otherwise unmarred sword. "Very bad. Who would buy such trash?"

"I would," Duncan said reverently, his hands itching to take up the weapon.

"Ha," Hamza said. "One day you will find your proper sword, if God wills it, and it will be better than *this*. My friend Aziz keeps the best of his wares within his tent."

"Is it that Hamza ibn Mohammed seeks a new sword to replace his own?" Aziz asked, with barely disguised eagerness. "By God, you may have your choice of any of my poor blades, and a racing camel too, in trade for it."

Duncan blinked again. He had never gotten a chance for a detailed examination of Hamza's sword—he was too interested in avoiding it, earlier—and all he could see of it at the moment was the hilt, a rough, L-shaped silver handle with a ring set in the end.

Hamza saw the look in MacLeod's eye and smiled.

"Is it permitted?" MacLeod asked.

For an instant the two locked gazes over the hilt of the sword. It was not merely a matter of a mortal law about arming a slave; for the two of them, it was more than that, more than one man lending another a look at a blade. It was a matter of asking, and receiving, an ultimate trust, backed by a greater risk than mortal men could know—though the ending might be the same; the sword would not care if the blood it drank was mortal or Immortal, if the death it caused was followed by an abyss or a Quickening.

"Aye, indeed," Hamza said at last. A murmur ran around the watching men, and they pressed closer. Duncan glanced over his shoulder, uncomfortable with how closely they stood to him. As a result he almost missed the smooth glide of the sword from its sheath. Warned by a too-familiar whisper of sound, he looked back to see the tip clearing the lip of the embroidered cover.

It was, to MacLeod's eye, an odd and rich blade: not straight, but curved, almost bent; the steel blue-and-gray; a wide channel the whole length of the weapon filled with arabesques and an inscription in the knotted Arabic script in bright gold; a blade wider toward the tip than the hilt—a scimitar.

He had never seen one quite like it. There was no bell, no handguard, only the thick hammered hilt and a pair of quillions, perpendicular to the grip. The metal glistened where it caught the sun; where it was not inlaid and inscribed, a regular pattern of blue, almost as regular and even as the scales of a fish, or the ripples of an ocean, covered it.

He couldn't miss Aziz's covetous gaze as Hamza, with only the barest of hesitations, handed the sword to him. The merchant wanted the sword more than his own life. "It is forbidden—" he began.

"On my head be it," Hamza said calmly.

"Ahhhhh," the assembled onlookers sighed, as Duncan lifted the blade.

Duncan MacLeod could not but agree with them. It was not merely that it was perfectly balanced. The sword of Hamza el Kahir was as a live thing, light and elegant, begging to be swung and slice the wind, to sing in his hand. He moved his arm, his wrist experimentally, and the audience, all except Hamza, moved back. Hamza alone remained where he was, easily within the radius of his swing, and watched Duncan, and smiled. Duncan glanced at him and set himself, raised his arm high and brought it down. It was as if he brought down his own arm, so much a part of him the sword felt.

And yet . . .

And yet, it was not *his* sword.

He swished it through the air a few more times, and then surrendered it, reluctantly.

"Where might a man find a sword like that?" he asked, unable to deny the yearning as Hamza sheathed the scimitar.

"Verily, there is no sword like that one," Aziz said. For a moment he and Duncan were in perfect accord, religious and cultural differences set aside out of respect for the perfect example of the swordsmith's art. "It is the Giver of Mercy, the Drinker of the Blood of Infidels, the Taker of Heads, the Daughter of Justice. It has been passed down in Hamza's family for generations, since the days of the great metalsmiths of Granada. It is a sword worthy of kings. It is said that whoever bears that sword will live forever."

The faintest of deprecating smiles played on Hamza's lips as he listened to Aziz.

Duncan drew a deep breath. He was already familiar with the most basic of mild deceptions practiced by Immortals; "passed down in his family" was the least of them. Hamza had made the sword himself. The legend that it bestowed immortality, though, was something else again. There were those who would believe it.

There were those who would seek to test it, for fear it might be true—

In the end, there can be only one—

"He is gifted, is he not?" Hamza said, referring to Duncan. Duncan couldn't tell if he was being modest about the scimitar, or leading into a negotiation.

Apparently Aziz thought the latter, and declined to participate. "You are an infidel," he said with regret. "And a slave. It is forbidden that such as you should have a weapon." He shook his head mournfully, carefully refraining from meeting Hamza's gaze to avoid the offense of refusing to deal with him. "You will not find a sword here, my friend. Though you may look, and try, you may not take. Our scimitars are not for you."

Chapter Seven

――――――

My lord Hamza has led Duncan MacLeod to Aziz the
merchant. I am informed by my brothers that Xavier
St. Cloud is hunting once again; it may be well that
MacLeod finds a decent sword. Though we are not
permitted to interfere; though MacLeod is an infidel,
and untried; still, it would be better if St. Cloud were
not the one remaining. We are not permitted to judge
them. Yet we know that one day we may be judged by
them. . . .

—el'Amin

In the end, Hamza purchased nothing. He and the merchant
engaged in animated discussion for quite some time while
Duncan continued to examine the various weapons, finding
none of them quite to his liking. It was easier to swing a
sword, he found, than to think about Terezia. Aziz and
Hamza allowed him to test the rest of the blades, even
though he would not be able to purchase one, and he welcomed the distraction. After a while the audience grew bored
at watching the European hack and thrust at nothing, his face
twisted with concentration, and wandered away.

D'Valenzuela would have laughed at him for a lovesick

puppy, but the thought of her immured in ibn Rais' mud palace lent strength to his arm. The swords sliced through the air, over and over, one after another. The curved blades lent themselves to cutting rather than thrusting, and were shorter than he was used to.

He attacked the image of the corsair, imagining him cut down as he had cut down so many: rival clansmen, English—any he was paid to. There were plenty who would hire a sword from a man who had nothing else to sell. People died so easily; one shove of metal just *there*, or *there*, or *there*—or there, across the neck, and the head of mortal or Immortal alike would go rolling across the desert sand.

He was good at killing. He had been employed at it for years. It was only lately, in his renewed lifetime, that he had begun to find polish, begun to think that perhaps he could be good at other things too.

He was not certain he could ever be good enough for someone like Terezia.

He blinked sweat out of his eyes and slashed madly at the empty air, staggering, gasping for breath.

"Enough, I think," Hamza said judiciously. "You are making a spectacle of yourself before the goats. It is too hot for such exercise. Come with me, and tell me yet again about this woman who obsesses you so."

"I don't know if it's Terezia, or just the thought of her," Duncan said helplessly. He and Hamza were circling each other in an empty white room tucked away in the back of Hamza's home, sparring with carved wooden versions of the curved swords in Aziz's stock. So far Duncan hadn't managed to touch the other man, though he himself had a nicely healing collection of welts and bruises on his arms, legs, body, and face. He wasn't certain whether his poor performance was due to his distraction or to his unfamiliarity with the weapon, though he had to concede that Hamza was very, very good.

"Women weaken men," Hamza said, cracking him across the shins.

Unable to stifle a yelp, Duncan glared at him. "Aye, is that so? And you with three wives?"

Hamza grinned. "Fortunate for you, isn't it?" *Whack.*

Duncan grinned back without humor and gathered himself. He was bigger than the other man, after all, he had carried a sword for more than fifty years—

And somehow his weapon was lying on the tiled floor, and he was on one knee, and his arm was numb from elbow to fingertips.

He stared at the wooden sword, then up at the other man. "It's a good thing you're who you are," he said wryly, "or it would be my head lying there."

Hamza saluted him and put up his sword. "Even so. Even such a modest gift as my own may be honed by years of practice. But you have talent, MacLeod. It will serve you well if you live to use it."

"So," he went on, recovering Duncan's sword and placing both weapons in a rack on a wall, "this Terezia, she is not one of us? You would have mentioned that, surely."

Duncan closed his eyes and shook his head. "No." He took a cotton cloth from a rack against the wall and wiped the sweat from his arms and chest.

"Then what does it matter, in the long run?" Hamza, having already dried himself, slipped the long cotton thobe over his head.

"Would you say the same of your wives?" MacLeod snapped. "Because we are Immortal, does that mean we cannot love?"

"It means that every mortal we love, we lose." Hamza shrugged. "I love each one of my wives dearly—I have loved all of them dearly. . . . I suppose I might do something rash to preserve them, though rashness is not a part of my nature." He touched the sheath of the scimitar with his fingertips, almost absentmindedly, affectionately. "You will find, Duncan MacLeod, that long life either gives that life great value, or no value at all." His voice was very soft, trailing off into nothingness. Duncan waited.

When Hamza resumed speaking, it was in an uncharacteristically practical, brisk tone. "Ibn Rais is very powerful in this city. He is high in the favor of the Sultan's Vizier. To take one of his captives from his own house is to risk one's head, and you will die the forever death—and all that you are will be lost with it." He raised one inquiring eyebrow.

"It is worth it," MacLeod said softly.

"If it is truly so, then, my infidel brother, let us consider seriously what you may do to recover this woman—and survive to enjoy the rewards of doing so."

In the light of the full moon, Algiers gleamed, a city of pearl and shadows. Hamza stood at MacLeod's shoulder in the alley behind ibn Rais' home, holding the single rein of a racing dromedary. A horsehair rope hung down from the crenellation of the house across the narrow way, a precise black line against the whiteness.

"I have not, of course, ever been within the women's quarters myself," Hamza was saying. "But all such are alike in many ways—the houses, I mean. So on the other side of this wall you will find a garden, and flowers. Ibn Rais has but one wife; you will find slaves, and guards. Because they came from Turkey, they will be eunuchs, but—" He hesitated, and his hand fell to the black scabbard at his side. "Take this. It will serve you well; you may not live forever, but you will live through this night, at least."

It was the Taker of Heads, the Daughter of Justice. Duncan slid his hand around the thick silver hilt and slid the blade free of the leather scabbard just enough to see the beginning of the inscription. "I canna take this," he whispered. "I canna leave you defenseless."

"It will inspire you to move quickly," Hamza said. He was already pressing himself against the far wall, into the shadows of the camel. "There are no others of us near. Go. Do what you must, and return quickly."

Unable to find the right words, Duncan gave him a long look instead, and held up the sword in salute. Hamza shook his head, deprecating. "Honor the sword, MacLeod, not me."

"I'll bring it back to you," he promised. Then he strapped it about his waist and swarmed up the rope without looking back.

From the top of the wall, it was an easy jump across the alley. Duncan crouched on the wall like a great cat, sparing one glance down at Hamza and the camel before looking into the garden.

He could smell the sweet perfume of orange trees, roses, grape vines; the stink of burning oil. He could hear the music of falling water, feel its cool touch as a physical caress. Blended into, yet beyond the sound of water, he could hear a stringed instrument, and the sound of feminine laughter.

The garden was a confusing place of shadows and moonlight. It was bounded by a row of rooms lit by lamps, glowing golden through windows in the doors. Immediately below him, lining the walls, were masses of rose bushes, their spicy, sweet scent filling his nostrils.

Leaping to the ground, he paused to catch his breath and listen again. Aside from the crickets, suddenly still, no one seemed to have heard the impact.

Now that he was actually inside the garden, he could see more clearly. There was an arbor, and marble benches were set around the fountain. The area was etched by an intricate knot of gravel paths setting off riotously blooming flowers, trees, even open patches of grass. He licked his lips and edged along the perimeter, keeping just clear of the thorny bushes.

The sound of the guitar and the flute were clearer now as he stopped opposite the fountain. Someone was singing a plaintive song—at least the song sounded plaintive; it was in a language he didn't understand, not Arabic. But the words seemed to amuse someone, because they were greeted with laughter, both from the audience and the singer. He was about to move closer when a shadow moved in the corner of the garden, low to the ground.

Duncan froze as a change in the direction of the wind brought a new scent to him, heavy, rank.

"Damn," he muttered to himself. "Why couldna it be eunuchs?" He spared an annoyed thought for Hamza, too, who had neglected to mention the other guardian of ibn Rais' women's quarters, a massive, black-maned lion.

A lion could not—he was nearly sure—take his head. It could kill him temporarily, though, and the process was certain to be unpleasant. The Daughter of Justice slid out of its sheath with a whisper of anticipation.

Singularly unimpressed, the lion sat in the middle of a pool of light and blinked at him, its eyes opaque with light reflected from the pool.

He had seen a lion once before, in a French zoo. It had been a sickly beast, ribs showing, half its teeth gone. He'd been impressed by the claws, though.

This lion was far from sickly-looking, even in moonlight, and—he noted as it yawned—it still had all its teeth. It was quite the magnificent animal, in fact, with a full wild black mane and solid slabs of muscle that shifted and flowed over its bones as it stood and stretched and rubbed its jaw against the ground. The animal stretched out its front paws and dug deep, deep into the gravel with claws the size of the curved daggers Aziz sold in the marketplace. Duncan swallowed dryly and raised the sword.

Standing again, the lion sniffed at the ground, dropped his shoulder, and rolled, scrubbing its back into the rucked-up earth with all the ecstasy of a house cat discovering a patch of catnip. Duncan stared in disbelief as the lion groaned and roared, exposing its belly, waving its huge paws in the air.

The music from the lighted rooms fell silent, as if the occupants had paused to listen. Moments later one of the doors opened, the light silhouetting a human figure. Duncan stepped back into the shadow of one of the orange trees. His movement caught the attention of the lion, and it twisted and leaped to its feet once again, sinking into a hunting crouch.

It was really quite amazing how much it resembled a hearth cat; Duncan had seen one slink in just such a fashion, belly to the ground, gaze fixed hard upon a mouse in the corner. Only now it was Duncan MacLeod who was the mouse, and the cat was twice his size.

The silhouette from the doorway stepped into the middle of the open area. The cat's tail lashed in irritation, and it oozed closer to Duncan.

The hearth cat used to twitch its hindquarters in just that way, before making its final rush to seize its prey. Duncan braced himself against the tree trunk, holding the sword before him. It would be too much to hope that the lion would run upon the scimitar as if it were a boar spear, but he had never fought a lion before, and he wasn't at all sure what else to do.

The silhouette was a man, a massive man—half a foot again taller than MacLeod. He wore only loose cotton breeches and a turban, and carried something in one hand, and while the earth did not quite shake at his passing, his footsteps were heavy enough to distract the lion. The cat raised and swiveled its head to look at the newcomer.

The guard's mass wasn't muscle; rolls of fat hung from his upper arms and sagged over his belt. The objects in his hands were chains, light ones that chimed together as his hand swung back and forth. The lion coughed, and suddenly Duncan was sure it had changed its selection of prey, that the unarmed man before him was doomed to die under the animals' claws and teeth. He drew a deep breath, preparing to step out and kill the animal before it could leap.

But the man—the eunuch—showed no fear as he called to the lion in a curiously high, sweet voice, raising the chains in his hand as if in invitation. The lion snarled, swung its head back toward MacLeod in indecision.

The eunuch peered into the shadow, trying to see what had attracted the big cat's attention without moving from his place. A sleepy nightingale called from a tree nearby, protesting. It snatched the cat's attention away from MacLeod, but in seeking the bird it took one long stride toward the trees that sheltered him as well.

The eunuch called again and rattled the chains coaxingly. The lion ignored him, freezing to find the nightingale again. The eunuch's voice took on a note of desperation, and he slapped the chain against the dirt. The lion's head swiveled back as the massive man dragged the chain enticingly in the gravel, and the animal snarled, its patience tested to the limit by the continuing distraction.

MacLeod would not have believed anything so large could move so quickly. The lion spun and leaped, pinning the chain, and kept going. Its next fluid leap brought the eunuch down. The man barely had a chance to scream before the cat's jaws closed over his head and *crunched*.

Chapter Eight

———

*St. Cloud has taken heads in Marrakesh; there are no
Immortals left where he has been. It is not yet time
for the Gathering, but when the madness takes him,
he kills. He has killed his Watcher too, though we do
not think he knew her for what she was; still, it was
ill done to have her marry him. He has too much
pride to answer questions from a woman . . .*

—el'Amin

The lion made a gagging, coughing noise that nearly covered
the wet, splintering sound of the skull collapsing, and shook
its head hard. There was a cracking sound, and the body
flopped back and forth as if it were suddenly weightless, as if
all the bones that gave it stature had turned to wax and
melted into the ground. It was too late to save the man;
MacLeod could not, though he was out of the shadows and
halfway across the open space before three more eunuchs
burst out of the room and threw themselves onto the animal.

Encumbered by its prey, the lion's first strike in its own
defense only raked one of the eunuchs from throat to crotch,
sending him reeling back wailing. It gave the other two time
to loop thin metal chains about the lion's thick-maned neck

as it tried to shake its jaws loose, and they retreated frantically in opposite directions as the animal roared and struck frantically to either side.

The chains were slender, meant for show, not for restraint. The men were unevenly matched. The lion spun and yanked one chain loose as MacLeod raised a Highland warcry and rushed in upon it, intercepting it in mid-rush as it lunged at the stronger of the two men.

The Daughter of Justice rose and fell as the lion rose, maddened, rising into the swordstroke. The sword caught the beast across the withers with a jar that nearly wrenched the weapon out of his hand. The cat screamed, a cry nearly as high as that of the eunuch collapsing under its weight, and shuddered, trying with severed muscles to turn and savage its new attacker. The remaining guard was scrabbling backward, away from the lion, from the avenging demon with the curved sword that slashed and glittered again, sending lion's blood spraying up against the moon.

The lion caught MacLeod across one arm with claws as long as his fingers, ripping it to the bone. MacLeod couldn't feel it. He was yelling still, the wild cry of the MacLeod clan, pushing back against the animal's fetid breath, drowning out its roars. Some remote part of his mind realized that the doors to the rooms surrounding the garden were all open now, filled with the figures of women; that the noise must surely bring forth whatever other men ibn Rais might have; that whatever hope he had ever had of moving secretly, quietly, to prize Terezia away from here was long since gone. Some remote part of his mind saw the bones of his own arm glistening, knew that there was pain. He could not take the time to assess his wounds. He could only strike again and again and again, until the lion fell back, its eyes still blazing contempt at the petty human thing which dared to raise itself up and deal out its death. It sagged back, finally, still snarling, claws still twitching uselessly, and it died.

He collapsed to his knees beside it, supporting himself on the blade-tip of the scimitar, his lungs heaving like bellows as he gasped for air. The roaring in his ears began to dim. It was, of a sudden, very quiet, except for his own panting. The air reeked of dying.

He raised his head, slowly, to look around, to see, with a visceral shudder, the shapeless crushed mass of the first guard's head nearly torn from his shoulders; the long dark-and-light body of the lion curled almost protectively around him, its lip still curled, exposing long reddened fangs; the other two eunuchs, one still sprawled on the ground, the other huddled under the orange tree; the women, standing in the doorways. It was a foolish thing for them to do, he thought. What if he hadn't been able to—

He slumped, a light moan escaping from his lips as the shock of it hit him. His arm was healing, of course—the flesh back in place as if nothing had ever happened, the bone decently hidden. He could pass off the blood as the lion's, but—it could have been *his* head. *His* life.

"Terezia?"

He had to swallow and try again before the name could be more than a noise. At least it was a noise that broke the silence; the women murmured excitedly to each other, their voices like bells. "Terezia?"

The third eunuch, recalled to his duty perhaps by the depth of MacLeod's voice, got to his feet and approached warily. Duncan looked at him, and he stepped back hastily.

"Terezia?"

"Duncan? Duncan MacLeod?"

It was Terezia, and he would not greet her on his knees. The blade of the sword bent alarmingly, but held, as he shoved himself upright again.

For a moment he couldn't tell which of the blurred figures before him was hers. They were gathered around chirruping like birds, adjusting the veils over their faces so that only their eyes were exposed. It seemed a great waste of energy, considering how light their clothing was; here, in the safety of their own quarters, they didn't bother with the all-enveloping robes.

One of them wasn't bothering even with the veil. And she had blue eyes, light brown hair, fair pale skin; she was dressed in a thin cotton gown, and looked like an angel without the wings. She was looking at him with terror and concern. "Duncan, you're hurt—"

"Och, no, it's nothing." He smiled. It was easier now; even the dizziness was fading. Pulling in a deep breath, he went on, "I came to fetch you out, my lady. I think—" He glanced about, grateful that the rest of ibn Rais' men had not yet put in an appearance. Perhaps they were constrained from appearing in the women's quarters? "I think we may be able to leave, if the guards will but look t'other way."

Mild confusion crossed her face, and he mentally cursed the richness of his native brogue. "Come awa' wi' me, lass." He held out his hand to her, expectantly.

Terezia did not, as he expected, as he hoped, fall weeping into his arms. Nor did she accept his proffered hand. She bit her lip—her full, luscious lower lip—instead, looking back at the other women. "I can't go with you, Duncan."

He stared at her, dumbfounded. "Are you mad? You can't *not* go." *Not after all this*, he nearly added.

But she was shaking her head, her eyes welling. "Duncan, you don't understand. I'm supposed to be here. It's all arranged."

"Arranged?" She was saying words, but they didn't have any meaning. He grabbed her arm, intending to shake sense into her.

"Duncan, don't. It's true. I arranged, in Venice, with the Turkish Ambassador. I am meeting—someone—here. My father would never have allowed it, so we had to set up a kidnapping—"

It made no sense. It was madness. "But d'Valenzuela died."

"I know. And it was dreadful. It wasn't supposed to happen that way. But it was the only way."

"You could have told us." He was aware of anger, deep inside, at the needless death of his friend; other than that he felt nothing at all. Her words washed over him like Mediterranean waves, warm but unable to sustain him. "You could have told me—"

"But I couldn't," she said desperately, running a small soft hand up his chest. For an instant he responded to the touch, until the giggles of the audience brought him back to where he was, and why. Terezia was looking up at him still, ignoring them, her eyes huge, dark, luminous in the moonlight. "I couldn't, Duncan. You'd never have allowed it. You wouldn't understand."

"Aye, you're right about that. I most certainly would not!" He glanced around at the assembled women. "I would not have permitted you to make such a ridiculous bargain; good men have died, and your own father, your brother—*I*"—he ground his teeth at the memory—"I was sold in the marketplace like someone's second-best horse, all for your 'arrangement'!

"Do you truly believe these corsairs will help you?" he snapped. "You're a prisoner here, you fool. You're ibn Rais' plaything. I'll bring you out of this place even if I have to carry you over my shoulder. Come away with me. Now."

"I will *not* come." Her hand, still resting flat against his chest, became rigid. "You're an honorable man, Duncan, but you don't understand. You see only corsairs and Moors and strangers—you're a mercenary, you only know fighting and killing. You don't know anything about love.

"Maybe you can carry me off over your shoulder, but if you do I'll find a way to get away from you and come back."

She was serious. She was absolutely serious. Duncan shook his head, amazed, and more than a little hurt by her words. "Who is it you're waiting for? Who do you think ibn Rais will turn you over to?"

"I will turn her over to no one," said ibn Rais, from the largest doorway.

The assembled women gasped and chattered, pulling away on either side until there was a path leading from Duncan, bloody and tattered, and Terezia and the dead lion, to the lord of the house, gorgeous in red silks and gold chains, with a very businesslike sword in his hand. MacLeod could scarcely recognize him as the filthy corsair who had taken the *Sancta Innocenta*. The man before him was, in his way, as noble in his bearing as any great lord of a Christian court.

Terezia stiffened under Duncan's hands, and then, incredibly, smiled, turned, and stepped out of his grasp to go to the pirate. Her glossy hair swung as she grasped his arm and turned back to Duncan.

"This is the man I met. This is the man I want to stay with."

Ibn Rais gestured to her to stand behind him, and she did so, immediately, obediently.

Duncan felt a shock of recognition. Dressed as he was here, in costly silk and gold, ibn Rais suddenly came into focus as someone Duncan had seen once before, far away and under very different circumstances, at a society function in Venice. Ibn Rais had been described to him—though not by name!—as an ambassador from the Turkish court. . . .

"Your father had arranged an honorable marriage for

you," he sputtered. "He took great care for you. Will you dishonor your family and your name in such a fashion?"

"My father never consulted *me* in the matter," the girl responded. "And he took more care for his family fortune by the marriage he arranged. You were sold in the slave markets of Algiers, Duncan MacLeod, but I was sold in the marriage markets of Christianity. I liked it no better than you. I met a man I loved, instead, in the Doge's court."

"Meanwhile," ibn Rais said silkily, "you are here, infidel, in a place no whole man but one may be. You have a choice before you, MacLeod."

He had an idea he knew what the choice was already, but he liked to be clear about these things. "And that might be?"

"You may surrender your manhood or your head." Ibn Rais lifted his sword suggestively. "But *my* honor requires one or the other."

Terezia made a sound of protest.

MacLeod agreed with her. It might be that his body could heal itself even of such a loss, but it was not an experiment he cared to subject himself to.

"I'll do neither one," he said, raising his own sword. "It'll be you dying, with your pet cat." He wondered, for one panicked instant, if Hamza, on the other side of the wall, would get his Quickening. The panic was replaced almost at once with an irrational certainty that no mere mortal, no man living, could take the head of Duncan MacLeod.

The Moor glanced at the body of the lion, limp and dark against the gravel path. Closer to him lay the savaged body of the eunuch. "That may be as God wills," ibn Rais said. "But even so, you would have to kill every person in this house in order to escape; you would never escape Algiers."

As he spoke, the other eunuchs crept out again, moving around MacLeod. He raised the bloody sword, warning them off.

"Where did you get that?" ibn Rais demanded, finally getting a good look at the weapon. "That sword belongs to your master, Hamza el Kahir. Are you a thief as well?"

"I am—" He started to say *I am no thief*, but that would implicate Hamza. At the same time, he could not admit to something that was not only not true, but shameful. He fell silent instead, watching as the eunuchs gathered their nerve for a final rush. The women had withdrawn to their rooms and were watching from the safety of the doorways. Even Terezia, he noted bitterly, had vanished.

"You say nothing, infidel? Do you then leave the choice up to me?" He indicated Hamza's sword with the tip of his own blade. "Drop that, you dog. It is an honorable weapon, not for the likes of you."

MacLeod swallowed, and then grinned suddenly. "Och, my mother always treated me like a laird. She'd be pleased to hear I at least had an honorable death."

"What are you saying?" said ibn Rais, not certain he was hearing the words correctly underneath the thick burr.

The eunuchs were closer now, poised to snatch at his arms.

"Ah, 'tis only that beheading's only for the nobility where I come from; the most honorable death. Did my family know you treated visitors to your women's quarters so well, you'd have Scots climbing your walls every night and half the day as well. And with only yon half-men to stop them, well—"

He was buried, then, under half a dozen outraged eunuchs, the sword torn from his hand even as he swung it. He tried to twist away from the grasping hands, to get free, but there was no escape. The gravel bit into his knees as he was forced to kneel before ibn Rais. Fingers twisted into his hair pulled back his head, exposing his throat; each arm was held hard, and a knee between his shoulders shoved him forward.

Ibn Rais stepped forward to pick up the discarded sword,

holding it up reverently to the light. "I shall make sure this is returned to its rightful owner," he said quietly. "But before I do so, I will cleanse it in your blood. You are an infidel, a thief, a despoiler of virgins. You have no right to carry an honorable blade such as this."

The Daughter of Justice caught the moonlight as he used it to lift Duncan's head even more, the inscription stark black against the gold. MacLeod could feel his pulse beating against the tip, the warm trickle of blood sliding down the outside of his throat. "Aye," he said, forcing himself to laugh, "but at least I'm not a murdering heathen pirate. And I'll die with great honor, no matter what you claim."

For a long moment their eyes met, Muslim lord and Scots mercenary, and then ibn Rais smiled in return. "Do you think so, infidel? For I do not."

The sword dropped, then rose again with terrifying suddenness. MacLeod could not restrain a scream as the scimitar slid deep into his breast. It was the shock, mostly; at first there was no pain at all, and then the blade found his heart and twisted, and there was nothing but pain and the dispassionate eyes of the man who killed him. He gasped, twice, seeking desperately past the sudden, shocking agony for air, for life—

The last thing he saw was the look of utter contempt on ibn Rais' face; and then came the blackness, the silence, the death.

Chapter Nine

*We are greatly concerned about the approach of the
Immortal Xavier St. Cloud. We are reluctant to
assign a new Watcher to him, yet we must observe
him; he may, after all, win through to the very end.
He already has a long history of challenges.*
  Ibn Rais has killed MacLeod.

—el'Amin

Ibn Rais had killed MacLeod.

He awoke from his death with a jerk and a gasp, trying
desperately to orient himself. Hamza el Kahir sat quietly in a
corner of the room, the ancient scimitar resting across his
thighs, watching him.

"What—where—"

"Peace, my friend. You are in my home." Hamza was
shaking his head, almost fondly. "I thought you were going
to rescue a woman. I did not expect to find your lifeless body
thrown over the garden wall, as if to the dogs. I nearly lost
the camel."

MacLeod was unable to stop himself from seeking the
wound that had killed him. It wasn't there; there was no
mark at all. There was not so much as a rent in his attire; the

blood had been cleaned away and he had been dressed in new, fresh clothing. He shivered, as much in reaction as anything else, as one hand drifted up to his throat, just to make sure his head was still attached.

"You are most fortunate," Hamza said, his hands unconsciously caressing the blade ever so lightly.

"Aye," MacLeod agreed fervently, sitting up. "I was sure he was going to take my head."

"I am surprised he did not."

"I think he didn't want to honor me so much."

"Ah." Hamza nodded, as if he understood, when clearly he did not. "A messenger from his house returned my sword, with the news that the thief who had stolen it had been dealt with. I was barely in time to receive the message." He sighed gently. "And the woman?"

"The woman . . ." Duncan was still feeling for the hole his memory told him ought to be in his chest. "The woman said she wanted to stay. I don't understand it."

"It is not given to us to understand all things," Hamza observed. "In any case, you are dead in this place; you will have to leave."

Duncan nodded reluctantly. "She doesn't belong there," he began.

"It is of no consequence now. You are dead, and the dead rescue no one. Especially those who have been given the opportunity and turned it down." He sighed. "I have returned the camel. You cannot remain in Algiers now, either.

"We will take horses, I think, to Tunis. You will rest for this day. We will leave tomorrow, after the morning prayer." He looked down at the sword. "I regret that this blade was used on you, my friend."

"I would have regretted it more if ibn Rais had taken my head with it," Duncan pointed out. "Hamza—"

The other man looked up.

"Thank you."

Hamza el Kahir smiled gently and rose to his feet, saluted Duncan, and left the room, leaving him to slam a frustrated fist against a stone wall.

The posting inns along the great trade routes of North Africa ranged from mere oases to small cities in their own right, with walls of whitewashed stone, stables and fodder for the hundreds of horses and camels transporting goods, places where travelers could refresh themselves, rest and wash and eat. It was quite civilized, really, MacLeod thought, except for the bloody endless sunshine.

They entered one of the open-air cafés, looking for food. They had missed joining a trade caravan that morning and had decided to take the opportunity to rest the horses a while longer. Hamza was looking at his watch, a large, round mechanism with an ornately inscribed face. He had a liking for such mechanical toys, though for the life of him Duncan couldn't understand why.

He and his mentor were still dressed in traveling robes, in shades of brown and white. Before they had left Algiers, Hamza had gotten MacLeod a sword, not unlike the broadsword he was used to; it was a distinct comfort to feel the weight at his side again, as if up until now he had been missing a vital piece of clothing.

They had hoped to make more progress today, though MacLeod hadn't been looking forward to another day on horseback. He hadn't slept well the previous night. He was tired and impatient, annoyed that they had missed their contact. He was still not convinced they really needed the protection of a large group of travelers, and he was sweating and itching and miserable. "Ah, this accursed heat," he muttered. "It must be noon already." His accent was thicker than usual with irritation, but he didn't care.

Hamza consulted the watch again. "It is 9:30, my friend. Still the cool part of the day." He snapped it shut with a smile.

MacLeod was in no mood to be appeased; he was still smarting from the rejection by Terezia and the need to leave Algiers. A dead man could not be seen in the city streets, after all. "What's the use of that thing? Counting minutes when we have forever. . . ."

Hamza shrugged, saluting the men at a nearby table. "It is all written. How long anyone has is in the hands of Allah. Besides, you Europeans invented minutes. Here there is only morning, noon, and night." They sat at a small table bearing bowls of olives and dates, and a serving man appeared almost instantly to pour two cups of steaming tea for them.

"Shook-ron," MacLeod muttered, thanking the serving man but still sulking.

"Patience, my friend. The desert teaches that, if nothing else. We'll leave for Tunis in the evening. Even we can't travel far in the midday sun."

MacLeod sipped, sputtered. "This is hot! What d'you want to drink that for? I want something cold!"

Hamza smiled again, sipping his own tea with obvious pleasure. "You miss this Scotland of yours?"

"Aye!" At the moment, MacLeod couldn't think of anywhere on earth he would rather be, in the chill mist of a Highland morning, with fog lying in the glens and sheep dotting the green hills. It had been too long since he had seen anything decently green. He was sick of North Africa, sick of the Mediterranean, sick of Algiers. He wanted to go *home*.

Hamza laughed. "Where it rains incessantly, and the people of your tribe eat grass?"

"Oats, Hamza, they eat oats. And aye, I could do with a bloody cold Highland ale right now." And the smell of a peat fire, and the skirl of pipes and the good songs of the Highlands—

Hamza raised his eyebrows, mildly affronted. MacLeod glared at him, exasperated. "What, you don't approve of my customs?" he asked sarcastically.

Hamza sighed gently. "Who can say? It is not for me to judge. Perhaps," he smiled wickedly, joking again, "one can *enjoy* eating the flesh of pigs and drinking vile concoctions."

MacLeod opened his mouth to respond and then shut it again. They could hear hoofbeats in the courtyard outside, and at the same time experienced sudden knowing, the certainty that there was another of their kind somewhere close. Hamza looked around behind himself, and both he and MacLeod saw the other at the same time.

A vaguely Oriental-looking black man of youthful appearance was standing there, brushing travel dust from black robes. He wore a curved, ornately inscribed scimitar at his side. He had sighted them too, and he was smiling, his eyes boring into theirs in blatant challenge.

"A Moor?" Duncan asked.

"A killer," Hamza responded, obviously recognizing the other man, and deeply shaken by it.

The newcomer strode over to the table, locking eyes with Hamza. "Hamza el Kahir," he said, not as a question.

"I have that honor," Hamza replied, with hard-held dignity. "You have traveled a long way."

"And you move quickly—for an old man." The newcomer's tone was mocking. His lips were curled in what might have been a smile, or a sneer.

MacLeod's temper snapped. "Keep a civil tongue in your head, if you want to keep it."

The other man looked MacLeod over, not quite smirking. He pretended to recoil in fear, holding out one hand. "Look, how I shake. My breath comes in labored gasps. What bravado!" Turning to Hamza, he inquired, "Who is this fool?"

Stung, MacLeod rose to his feet. "I am Duncan MacLeod of the Clan MacLeod."

The newcomer was still addressing Hamza, ignoring Duncan as if he were a child not yet breeched. "Does he always speak for you?"

To Duncan's surprise and fury, Hamza responded to the newcomer as if he agreed. "Forget him. He is too young for you to be concerned with."

"I am old enough to take his head!"

The man in black looked at him again and shrugged. "I don't sleep with virgins and I don't kill children."

Infuriated, MacLeod lunged, dragging at the sword Hamza had acquired for him the morning they had left Algiers.

Hamza stepped in his way, restraining him. "Not here!" he said quietly, urgently. "We are not alone!" Indeed, the other customers in the small café were watching the exchange among the three men with open curiosity. The third Immortal stood watching, amused rather than impressed.

"Then I will take it elsewhere," MacLeod said between his teeth, leaning heavily on the double entendre. The urge to wipe that smirk off the stranger's face, and with it his own accumulated frustration, was nearly overwhelming.

Hamza, still interposed between the two, kept trying to calm him. "It is not your concern!"

Duncan shot him a look of disbelief, as the stranger, still ignoring him, said to Hamza, "We will meet in two hours. The Square in the old quarter."

"He will be there," MacLeod snapped. *And so will Duncan MacLeod,* he thought, *and cheering Hamza on as he takes yon arrogant head.*

The stranger's head swiveled, and he looked at Duncan directly, and smiled. "Good. Because if he isn't—I'll come looking for *you*."

A sudden chill settled in MacLeod's gut, and he knew suddenly what birds in the nest must feel like when a snake comes slithering down the branch and pauses to look them over, selecting the first to devour at leisure. The stab of dread made him, irrationally, angrier still at this man who failed to show his friend the proper respect. "Anytime," he responded with all the bravado he could muster.

The other Immortal saw it for what it was. He laughed, then turned and strode out of the little café, leaving the two, along with the rest of the place's patrons, staring after him.

"Who is that camel dung?" MacLeod snarled.

Hamza was still staring after the other man, his face very pale. "Xavier St. Cloud," he answered abruptly.

MacLeod blinked. "A Christian name for a Moor?"

"He has been many things." The answer was almost absentminded, as if he were thinking of something else entirely.

MacLeod snorted. "Soon he'll be dead. You will show him what Damascus steel can do."

Hamza remained silent for a long moment, and then, as if coming to a decision, he said, "Finish your tea, and get the horses. It is time for us to go."

MacLeod stared at him in disbelief. This was not the Hamza he knew; nor was this the kind of behavior he could comprehend. He could understand fear, yes, though a man didn't admit to such a thing; he drank whisky if he needed more courage in his gut, and shouted louder and fought harder for it. But what Hamza seemed to be suggesting was—"You're going to *run*?"

It couldn't be. Running was what cowards did. And Hamza was not a coward.

"Would you rather I commit suicide?" the other man returned abruptly. Small beads of sweat stood out on his skin between the fold of his turban and his brows. He kept glancing back at the courtyard, as if he expected St. Cloud to appear again, sword at the ready despite the protective presence of mortals.

MacLeod was completely bewildered. Suicide? Hamza? "But I've seen you fight. You're *good*." He could still remember the numbness in his arm where the practice sword had hit a nerve, disarming him almost casually. He had considered himself experienced, until encountering Hamza el Kahir. He couldn't imagine anyone better.

The other man shook his head grimly, reaching for the silver cup on the table. "Not as good as Xavier. A man must know his limitations if he wants to survive." Draining the rest of his tea, he added, "We'll ride now. Lose him in the desert."

"Then you'll ride alone," MacLeod responded, outraged, as Hamza started for the archway.

Furious, frightened, desperate, the other man turned back, shaking a finger in MacLeod's face. "Xavier was right. You *are* a fool! You are too young, you have never fought one like this!"

A kind of arrogant madness seized him, and MacLeod heard himself say, "And he's never fought one like *me*. Not everything is written, Hamza. Ride on if you must—but *I* will stay." He flung himself back into the chair and reached for his own cup of rapidly cooling tea.

Hamza looked at him with resigned sorrow and saluted, the full, graceful salute of fingers to breast, lips, forehead. "Then may Allah be with you."

It was farewell, and he didn't want it; he wanted things to go back to how they had been, perhaps twenty minutes before as measured by Hamza's beloved watch. But he couldn't turn back time; he couldn't walk away from his own word, or a fight. "Aye," he said abruptly, not meeting the other man's eyes. "And with you."

Hamza paused for just an instant, as if to say something more, and then changed his mind and left, disappearing around the corner of the open wall of the café. MacLeod knocked back the remainder of his tea, absentmindedly grimacing at the taste. He was beginning to wish he had gone with the other man after all, but it was too late. He had given his word that he would stay and fight in his friend's place. It occurred to him suddenly that perhaps Hamza was right, and he might have agreed to die in Hamza's place. He couldn't decide, for the moment, whether it was "written" that way or not—but events would occur as *he* had said they would, or his name was not Duncan MacLeod.

The maze of passages that led to "the Square in the old quarter" of the caravanseri gave MacLeod a sense of comforting familiarity by now; he could almost have been back in Algiers, back before any of this madness had happened. The only difference was that in Algiers he had been unarmed, vulnerable. Now he carried a sword, and with it memories of all the battles he had fought in more than sixty years. He had survived them all. One way or another, he survived. . . .

An abrupt turn, and he stood at the end of the alley leading to the empty space, hand on the round pommel as he scanned, looking for St. Cloud. The square, in an abandoned section of the caravanseri, was open on one side to the empty desert. There was no sign or sense of another Immortal present.

"Xavier," he bellowed. "Are you going to keep me waiting all day?"

For an instant he wondered, with a guilty sense of hope, if

St. Cloud had thought better of the challenge. He had not, after all, fought anyone like MacLeod before—

But then the knowledge came, and without his conscious volition his hand gripped the hilt of the sword and pulled the weapon free of its scabbard with a deadly whisper of metal against metal. His body shifted into that peculiar combination of readiness and relaxation that was fighting-balance, and his nostrils flared as if seeking a scent. He could feel each individual grain of sand shifting beneath his sandals, taste the dry remnants of his own sweat on his lips—

He entered the square, and there to one side stood the dark man, waiting, a blot of depthless shadow against the white sand and white walls. The presence was very strong now, beating against his senses. For just an instant, his vision blurred as his heart accelerated at the sight of his enemy.

St. Cloud's hands were empty, hooked over his belt. He looked MacLeod over as if he had never seen anything quite like him before, and had not yet decided what to make of him.

"Such rudeness," he remarked calmly, glancing disdainfully at the drawn sword. "It must be Duncan MacLeod of the Clan MacLeod?"

The man's attitude took MacLeod aback. "Aye, it is, you arrogant pompous boor. Och, no, it's *Moor*, isn't it?" It was a weak reply, reeking of false bravado, but the best he could come up with at the moment.

"I was expecting Hamza." St. Cloud's imperturbable manner did not change.

"Wrong again," MacLeod sneered. He could take the man now, he thought—but no. St. Cloud had still not drawn his sword. It would not be honorable.

"Just how old are you?" his opponent inquired. "Are you a Christian or do you paint yourself blue and bay at the moon?"

MacLeod was taken aback. He hadn't planned for a religious discussion. "What do you care?"

"Just wondering what God I'll be sending you to." The other man smiled, and reached for his sword at last.

"Look to your own," he responded, and assumed his stance, raising the sword to guard. He wasn't afraid anymore. He was ready.

They were balanced, poised, when a new voice broke into their concentration, and both men abruptly realized that another Immortal had walked into their duel. "Xavier!"

It was Hamza, standing in the alleyway, his hand on the silver hilt of the Daughter of Justice. He was looking at MacLeod, an expression of resignation on his face, but his words were addressed to St. Cloud.

"Your challenge was to me," he said quietly. "And I accept."

"But I am ready!" MacLeod protested. It wasn't right; the fight had begun, even if no blows had yet been exchanged; and Hamza had been afraid, to the point of flight. The challenge had shifted; Hamza had no business trying to take it up in his place. The fact that he had effectively done exactly the same thing for Hamza was irrelevant. Swords had been drawn now.

He stepped forward, thinking he could talk Hamza out of it, delay St. Cloud so that his friend could still escape—

Hamza shook his head quietly. "It was always *my* fight." He looked at St. Cloud, let go a long breath of acknowledgment, of acceptance. What was written, was written. "It is done."

St. Cloud put up his sword, indicating the gap in the wall that led to open desert. He gave MacLeod a feral smile. "Look and listen, my pale friend. Your time will come."

MacLeod pulled close to Hamza, frustrated and dismayed.

"Why!" he demanded angrily. "And do not tell me it was written!"

Hamza regarded him with sadness, reaching up to grasp his shoulder in a grip that was not quite an embrace. "Because I cannot allow a friend to die in my place," he said quietly. He took the great watch from his robes and folded MacLeod's hands around it, capturing them tightly between the warmth of his own, living flesh and the cold, insensitive metal, and stared into MacLeod's eyes, as if trying to imprint the moment into the other man's mind forever. "Remember me," he murmured.

Then he turned, and without looking back, followed St. Cloud out into the desert.

Chapter Ten

Joe Dawson sat quietly for a long time, staring unseeing at the faded writing on the pages of the journal. Even after all these centuries, the flavor of the original Watchers' personalities still came through. Some of them sounded as if they hadn't much liked Immortals, or at least the young, brash, impetuous Immortal Duncan MacLeod had been back in those days.

Some had observed his activities with much the same sense of almost paternal fondness that Dawson himself did. And some had barely noticed him at all, assuming, perhaps, that Duncan MacLeod was but a minor player in the Game, soon to lose his head and be forgotten. Dawson smiled. MacLeod had survived, and grown, since the days of Hamza el Kahir.

He wondered if MacLeod had loved Terezia, or thought he did. Dawson couldn't recall any other mention of her in the records. Had he been young enough, still, to forget he was Immortal? Had he had hopes of sharing his life with her? The records could record only what the Watchers saw—not how the participants felt about it.

Shivering suddenly at the thought, he got awkwardly to his feet—sitting for long periods made walking more difficult—and moved over to the kitchen. There was a certain comfort in such mundane domestic tasks as preparing the coffeepot, heating water, waiting for it to filter while he puttered around, setting up some music on the CD player. It was quiet. Peaceful. Relaxing.

A breath of rum in his coffee. Some Charlie Parker. A good reading light. A comfortable chair. A good place, surrounded by his books, his music, work that could occupy his heart and mind. He lifted his feet one after the other to the ottoman, sipped at his coffee, and picked up the old journal again, handling it with affectionate respect.

This was a safe and comfortable exploration of the past, like reading the last pages of a mystery, where you knew the hero would survive falling off a cliff. In this case, he'd met the hero, so Dawson knew he'd survived. The tale, in a sense, wasn't so much about the man as it was the sword—the scimitar, come into Duncan's life once again.

What was it like to feel a blade like that, already blackened with the blood of a lion, being plunged into your heart, and twisted with brutal efficiency? Not for the first time, and likely not for the last, Joe Dawson experienced a flash of gratitude that he was merely mortal, and had only one death to die. Perhaps those ancient Watchers, his brothers and sisters, colleagues across the centuries, had felt the same way, Watching the same man—the same Immortal. Perhaps they too had felt the occasional flash of envy, balanced by pity, for those who lived forever, and lost so much in doing so.

The scimitar had to be Hamza's sword. For a time he'd thought it might be Xavier's, but no; that heavy silver hilt was unmistakable. Hamza's Watcher had described it in loving detail, and it matched the description, far more terse but just as evocative, provided by an earlier Watcher even longer ago. The ring in the cap, the shape of the hilt, and most of all the inscription, naming the sword and honoring the Prophet, and giving the "genealogy" of its maker and owner, all named it Hamza's. The Daughter of Justice. The Taker of Heads. Giver of Mercy.

Dawson shuddered.

Hamza el Kahir had been born in the time of Mohammed, in the holy city of Makkah. He had been one of the earliest followers of the monotheistic religion that had replaced the many gods of Arabia; he had died his first death in battle for Allah.

When he woke from that death, he had remained firm in his joyous submission to his God, even if he had been temporarily denied his promised Paradise. He had gone to Damascus and learned the art of swordsmithing, "died" many times, and finally taken his skills to the Iberian peninsula. He had spent nearly two centuries there, perfecting his craft, absorbing, contributing to, becoming a part of the high culture of Muslim Spain.

When the Moors had been driven out, he had settled in Rabat, and then Algiers. There he had lived unobtrusively, a teacher of swordsmanship to the young men, a writer of elegant poetry, and the benefactor of another of his kind, a young Christian captured as a slave. Not far from that city he had died the only death that counted for an Immortal, losing his head to Xavier St. Cloud.

None of his poems survived. Once he was gone, all he left behind him were journals like these, and perhaps one or two other bits and pieces his friends had associated with him. For all his more than seven centuries of life, Hamza el Kahir had left no lasting mark on human history.

Dawson hoped he had finally achieved his Paradise, his endless garden. All of the Watchers who had observed him wrote of him with respect, citing his chivalry and his skill. He had been a wise man, a good man, and finally, a brave and honorable one. MacLeod had been very lucky in Algiers. It was no wonder Hamza's sword had a special meaning for him.

Joe closed the journal and looked up at the bookshelves. There were many of them, packed with volume upon volume of leather-bound books, each branded with the circle and trefoil of the Watchers from time memorialized—life after life, the fleeting ones of Watchers recording the sometimes equally fleeting ones of the so-called Immortals.

The identities of the individual Watchers hadn't always survived. Their identities didn't matter; only their work. The Watchers were charged to observe, to record, and to remain hidden. Often they faded into the dust of history. Joe wondered how many of them had forged secret alliances with their subjects—how many Watchers had actually made friends with the Immortals they Watched. Surely he wasn't, in all of history, the only one?

If any of them had, the journals were silent on the subject. His relationship with MacLeod might really be unique. He didn't suppose he'd ever know. Certainly the Watcher who had witnessed MacLeod's fight with the lion was no friend to him.

MacLeod had been very young then. One had to be, in order to face a full-grown lion with nothing but a sword. Young, and crazy. Immortal or not, death by evisceration *had* to hurt; anyone with sense would give the animal a wide berth.

There had been another occasion, surely, in which a scimitar with a rough silver hilt had appeared? He drained the rest of the coffee and set the cup aside, struggled back to his feet. The Algerian journal was carefully set back in its proper place. His hand danced across several more, fingertips brushing lightly against the bindings until he found the one he wanted. Flipping through the book rapidly, he found the section he remembered, and he smiled to himself. More coffee was called for; it had been a long time since he'd read this, and he'd never expected to actually *see* the sword. . . .

Chapter Eleven

Cairo, December 1916 . . .

There is much excitement in Headquarters; Lawrence returned from the desert seeking supplies for the Arab army, and has been asked to consult with Colonel Clayton on the task force charged with the feasibility study of operations behind Turkish lines in the Arabian peninsula. He is a friend of MacLeod's, which makes my task even more interesting.

I have notified the appropriate personnel in case Lawrence finally persuades MacLeod to join him in the field. If he does, it is my hope that the Immortal manages to avoid capture; contacts at this time with our fellow Watchers in enemy forces would be viewed with the gravest suspicion by superior officers on both sides.

> —Lt. the Hon. Chas. Worthington Bracecourt
> Harrington-Smythe

"Faisal's army is in Yenbo, eight thousand men. We plan to move up the coast." A long finger tapped at a map of the Arabian peninsula. "Our ultimate objective, of course, is

Damascus, but first we have to take Agaba, and in order to do *that*—" The speaker shook his head. "Bremond wants a joint British/French expeditionary force. I tell you, sir, it won't work; the tribes will view it as an invasion. They'll just as likely turn on our army as attack the Turks."

Duncan MacLeod leaned unobtrusively against the wall in the back of the room, watching the four men gathered around the table. Two of them, wearing the precisely pressed khaki uniforms of British officers new to the Middle Eastern theatre—Duncan had mentally dubbed them Tweedledum and Tweedledee—were casting sidelong glances at the other two, paying far more attention to them than to the paper spread out before them.

Of the others, one wore the insignia of a colonel on his uniform. He studied the map with great interest. Dum and Dee stood slightly behind and to either side of him, radiating deference.

The last man standing at the table was dressed in the brown and white robes and headcloth of a Bedu tribesman, with bandoliers of ammunition crossed over his chest and an elaborately jeweled curved knife thrust into his belt. He was short, not more than five feet four inches, and wiry. It was his voice, in the cultivated accents of Oxford, that held their attention.

Duncan had been asked to deliver the maps from the depths of the Arab Bureau offices to Colonel Clayton's office. He remained because he was curious. For an accidental recruit in a war even less rational than most, the situation had elements of interest, particularly in this part of the world.

Long fingers of twilight painted gold through the high arched windows of the room, setting dust motes dancing. Headquarters Cairo was a yellow stone building with high ceilings and arched doorways and floors that rang to the boots of military men. Duncan couldn't decide whether the man in the traditional Bedouin robes, with the refined university accent, was any more out of place than the khaki-clad British military or not.

"What do you suggest, then, Captain? Oh yes, I did tell you you were a captain now, didn't I, Lawrence?" The colonel was speaking.

The soft refined voice was gratified. "No, sir. Thank you, sir."

"Not bad for a chap who 'likes things better than people,' eh?" The colonel, quoting back at Lawrence a phrase the smaller man had once used to describe himself, was obviously pleased. The other two officers glanced at each other. The expressions on their faces showed their thoughts as if they'd shouted them: they were confused, appalled at the idea that a British officer would voluntarily forsake His Majesty's uniform for the sake of Arab robes. Duncan crossed his arms and smiled to himself. The new ones always took some time to adjust.

"To answer your question, sir, I believe the Arab tribes should take the burden and the responsibility for their own independence. Faisal has an army; let him use it. What they need is supplies. Arms. Gold."

The two officers exchanged glances again. "Come now, Lawrence," Tweedledum said. "The tribes are a disorganized collection of petty sheikhs. They're fighting among themselves as much as they are against the Turks. Faisal may have enough of them to make a show at Yenbo, but that's just some religious thing because of his father—"

"Excuse me, sir," Lawrence interrupted. "Faisal's father is the Emir Hussein, Sherif of Mecca. He's the spiritual leader of most of Islam. And it is not just 'some religious thing'—it is the core of the Muslim existence."

"Then why are they still feuding with each other?" the other officer sniped. "If he's such an important leader—"

The newly made captain in the robes of a desert tribesman took a deep breath. "We are still introducing the concept of nationhood."

"How do you propose to use these supplies?" Clayton interrupted, ignoring his staff officers.

Lawrence took the change of subject gratefully. "Tribal leaders are pouring into Yenbo, offering allegiance to the Emir through his son. Some in the north are closer to the Turkish sphere of influence, and of course they're less likely to commit openly. However, as we move up the coast, we'll need their support. There are several sheikhs whose allegiance it's vital to have." The fingers tapped several areas on the map again. "The area here, in the north toward Syria, is the territory of the eastern Howeitat. Their chief, Auda abu Tayi, is definitely with us. However, there are several smaller tribes whose support may be pivotal. Those are the sheikhs whose confidence we must have. The Rushallah, the Beni Katib—"

"And how do you propose to get it?" one of the staff officers asked, clearly bored by the discussion. "They're out there in the desert, flitting about like a set of bloody will-o'-the-wisps. You can't even find them."

Lawrence straightened, folding his hands over the hilt of the curved dagger stuck into his belt. "Not necessarily, sir," he said mildly.

He wasn't a tall man, but he had presence when he chose to use it. He chose to now. The two staff officers were clearly baffled by the man with the fair skin and the bright blue eyes that stared so calmly from beneath kaffiyeh and agal.

"What d'you mean, 'not necessarily'? It's true!"

"Simple logic tells us that the movement of nomadic peoples is actually extremely restricted." The tone would, if one closed one's eyes, make a hearer think he was in a lecture hall at Kings or Magdalen. "The location of a given tribe is not an insurmountable problem."

Duncan smothered a chuckle.

Tweedledee heard it and decided to use MacLeod as a distraction from his own embarrassment. He spun smartly on his heel and pointed a riding crop at MacLeod. "Simple logic, eh? If it's that simple, pr'aps your messenger here can take over your lecture."

Lawrence turned to MacLeod, and a spark of humor danced in his gaze. "Perhaps so. MacLeod, would you care to take a stab at it?"

MacLeod didn't bother to hide his answering grin. His response was in a tone equally academic. "Nomads are bound by the needs of their herds, sir. They have to have water and feed. They'll exhaust the grazing ground at one oasis and move on to the next. The migration routes aren't too difficult to determine, given enough information about the types of animals they own and the water rights of a given tribe."

Clayton raised an eyebrow. "You seem quite knowledgeable, soldier."

Duncan almost shrugged, remembering just in time that the gesture was probably not appropriate while in uniform. At least not in the presence of a colonel. And while normally he wouldn't give a fig for a uniform *or* a colonel, in this case it was a matter of observing the customs of the country: It was good manners. "Thank you, sir." He didn't dare glance at the man in the Bedu robes, for fear of bursting out laughing.

"MacLeod has been with the Arab Bureau for some time, Colonel," Lawrence added, to fill the little silence that formed when Clayton waited for more information. "He is fluent in the language and customs of the people. In fact, I might even suggest"— the blue eyes had sharpened, become calculating—"MacLeod might be an excellent choice to send behind the lines to persuade one or two of those sheikhs I mentioned earlier."

That yanked MacLeod out of his amusement at Dee's discomfiture. *"What?"*

Colonel Clayton gave him a chilling glance. "I believe one of your superiors was speaking, soldier."

MacLeod bit back a response and tried to look abashed, meanwhile entertaining grim plans for Lawrence once he got him alone.

"What's the bloody Arab Bureau?" Dee snarled. "I don't recall seeing it in the Table of Organization."

Dum, eager to show off his greater knowledge, smirked. "It's that little research group Lawrence here put together. Publishes a brief analyzing the Turks and what they're really thinking and doing. Quite informative, really, considering its limitations—"

"The Arab Bulletin, yes," Lawrence said. He was, Duncan noted, becoming angry, though it was likely no one else in the room knew him well enough to realize what that particular tone meant.

"So you think someone ought to go talk to the tribes? I think that's a superb idea, don-cha-know," Dum said, trying to make up the ground. "Send this MacLeod chappie out and snaffle up some of 'em."

Lawrence had had enough. He stepped back from the table and turned to the colonel, indicating the discussion was over. "With your permission, sir, I'll make the arrangements. Meanwhile, I need to fill a requisition list and return to Yenbo as soon as possible. We want to encourage Faisal in his drive up the coast. Oh, and I'll need your authorization for the explosives—"

Duncan MacLeod had been minding his own business in the marbled halls of the Arab Bureau, not exactly military and not exactly not, for several months. Technically, he was a driver, chauffeuring ranking officers from place to place. In between times he amused himself tracking down the bits and scraps and pieces of intelligence and geography that, put together, made a mosaic of Turkish movements and strength.

He was good at it, nearly as good as the original editor of the Arab Bulletin. It was how he had come to meet Lawrence to begin with. He found himself liking the odd little archaeologist; before Lawrence had disappeared into the desert, they had had a number of interesting conversations about Arab history and customs and politics.

But that didn't mean he particularly wanted to go out into the desert himself. "What in bloody hell possessed you?" MacLeod snapped as he escorted the newly made Captain back to the obscure offices of the Arab Bureau. "That's your sort of thing, not mine!"

Lawrence smiled and nodded to a gaggle of officers as they passed, enjoying the shock on their faces as they tried to absorb, first, the presence of an apparent desert tribesman in their midst and second, the fact that the "tribesman's" face was unsettlingly familiar. "Oh, why not, MacLeod? It's only a little run into the Nefud. Find ibn Ashraf of the Rushallah—he's one of the keys, I think—and give him gold to join Faisal. You ought to find us at Um Lejj by that time; I don't think we'll have quite made it to Wedj. And then back here in time for tea. Nothing to it."

By this time they had entered the shadowy rooms occupied by the Bureau. The walls were papered with maps of the Middle East; file cabinets bulged with reports, and half a dozen personnel were typing up situation reports and copies of the latest edition of the *Bulletin* for high-level briefings.

MacLeod watched as Lawrence exchanged greetings with others who worked there, compiling intelligence information about the movements of the Turks and their interactions with the Bedouin tribes they fondly believed they ruled. Then they had to go through the obligatory round of congratulations on Lawrence's new rank. MacLeod waited until they were done and Lawrence had pulled out a set of maps, annotating them furiously in his angular, rapid handwriting.

"Oh, certainly," Duncan said sarcastically, when they could resume the conversation. "And what about the Saudis and their Wahhabis?" The Saudis, in the northwestern part of the Arabian peninsula, led the conservative Wahhabi faction, and were at odds with Sherif Hussein, the Emir of Mecca, often fighting him openly. Both sides were competing for British support. Lawrence openly favored the Emir and his sons, particularly Faisal, in the political struggle.

"Oh, I'm certain you can avoid them. It shouldn't be difficult to predict their movements either." Lawrence grinned.

"Oh, nothing to it," MacLeod agreed. "Thank you very much, Captain. It's just what I wanted, to go haring off. Not everyone enjoys that sort of thing, you know."

Lawrence smiled, not fooled by the disclaimer. "There's nothing for it, MacLeod. You'll have to go. We'll find a guide for you into the desert, and pack up the gold." He looked up from his writing, his blue eyes steady on the Immortal's brown ones. "There's no one else here I'd trust to do it properly, you know," he said. "You know them. You don't make a fuss about the robes. You know how to behave. I'd do it myself if there wasn't so much else to be done. And if we don't, Bremond is going to lead his army in after all, and you know what will happen if he does."

For one exasperated instant MacLeod wanted to ask the other man why he believed he was the only one who could successfully act as liaison to the desert Arabs—there were others with experience, after all—but it was a moot point. And Lawrence had conceded it anyway by his own words.

MacLeod sighed. "Oh, very well. I'll see if I can find something for you to blow up when you get there, shall I?"

Lawrence laughed. "Oh yes, please do. I'll even let you help if you like."

Duncan shook his head. "I don't think so, Captain. That particular pleasure can remain all yours." He paused before going on. "I'll do it, of course. But when I get back, perhaps you could put in a word for me; I'd like to get back somewhere where it snows occasionally."

Lawrence looked disappointed. "If you must, I suppose I could see. But you could just as easily get a promotion out of it. You're a dreadful waste of talent as a driver, MacLeod."

Declining to debate the point, MacLeod saluted, ironically, fingertips to breastbone, lips, forehead. "May Allah be with you in all your endeavors," he said in flawless, if somewhat archaic, Arabic.

"And with you, Duncan MacLeod," Lawrence answered in the same language, resigned. "And with you."

Chapter Twelve

Communication in wartime remains difficult. There
will always be a conflict of interest at such times
between those united by a common duty and divided
by opposing loyalties. It is my hope that this war ends
quickly, not only for the sake of those whose lives are
at risk but for those whose lives are not.
—Harrington-Smythe

The desert was still bloody hot, MacLeod thought, even in
winter. Except at night, when it was bloody cold. It was
enough to drive a man mad. He loosened the hem of the robe
around his neck.

And it had been a long time since he'd had to ride a camel.
They still stank, though, and this one had a tick the size of a
golf ball embedded behind its right ear; the beast's temper
was uncertain at best, and the constant pain couldn't be helping. MacLeod felt a flash of nausea every time he happened
to see the insect. Once they made the oasis, he promised
himself, he'd see it removed if he had to do it himself.

Meanwhile they swayed onward, he and his guide,
through endless vistas of sand like a rolling sea. Headquarters had considered the possibility of a full escort for the two

hundred pounds of gold Duncan was responsible for; either Tweedledum or Tweedledee had decided that he would be far less conspicuous with only a single guide—hoping, he suspected, that he'd lose it all. Lawrence had already left, and wasn't around to provide an officer's and expert's opinion.

The staff wasn't interested in what MacLeod had to say. He had been given the gold and the robes, and sent on his way. He had assumed Arab robes, without protest; they were much cooler and much less conspicuous than a British military uniform, and unlike some of the staff assigned to the Bureau, he had no distaste for them. That, with his knowledge of the language and people, allowed him to blend in better than, say, Tweedledum or Dee. He had travelled down one horn of the Red Sea and across its width by dhow, and now travelled by ship of the desert, looking for an elusive tribe to lure to the cause of the Arab revolt. At that point he had found a guide, a wizened little man named Ali ibn Jehail, recommended by the cousin of a brother of a clansman of a tribe allied to the cause of the Revolt. This was as good a job reference as Duncan was likely to get, given the population of this tiny settlement. He hadn't told the man why he wanted to find the Rushallah, and hadn't told him about the contents of the saddlebags.

So far, matters had gone fairly uneventfully. The camel's pace rocked him like a baby in a cradle; if it weren't for the heat, it would be easy to nod off, sleep the trip away.

No such luck, though. It was getting late. Before long they'd have to find some convenient dune and make camp for the heat of the day, get what rest they could. Then go onward, endlessly, searching the vast emptiness for some sign of life . . .

Something other than camels, and ticks, and a Bedouin guide who, MacLeod suspected, had no more idea than he himself did about where the Rushallah wells were. Despite his and Lawrence's academic posturing, *nobody* knew for certain anymore; there was too much disruption in northern Arabia these days. Oases that had been the property of particular tribes for generations had changed hands over and over as the Turks attempted to bring them under control.

It was nonsense, all of it. MacLeod was beginning to think he'd never see a war that actually made sense, no matter how long he lived. If he ever did, he hoped there wouldn't be any deserts involved. He was really getting tired of sand. It got into everything, even in Cairo; filming the tables, sifting into clothing, getting into teeth and hair. And it was even worse out in the desert.

The camel snorted, clearing sand from its nostrils. For a moment MacLeod envied the animal the ability, and then his glance fell on the tick again, and he shuddered in disgust.

He supposed that it made more sense to the British commanders in Delhi and Cairo and London to follow up on the bizarre plans of a young archaeologist with a penchant for dressing up than to commit men and matériel to a very secondary theatre of combat. Let the Arabs fight their own battles, and when it was all over—

One school of thought felt the Arabs would be too much trouble to colonize. Another saw them as part of the Empire, nations in their own right as much as Canada or Australia. A third didn't much care, as long as neither Russia nor France ended up with more influence than Britain did. He suspected that in the final analysis, Lawrence fell somewhere between the latter two positions.

Duncan MacLeod didn't much care. All he wanted to do was deliver his message and his gold and go back to Cairo— and if he was particularly fortunate and Lawrence kept his promise, to Europe. What did he care for the tangled alliances and ancient enmities that had plunged a whole world into yet another stupid, senseless conflagration? Nothing.

The camel swayed onward, caring even less than he did about a world war.

Up ahead of him, the mass of black perched upon the other camel turned about, revealing a grinning face ornamented by a gleaming gold tooth. "You are still here, English?"

"I am not English," MacLeod yelled back hoarsely, for the fourth time in two days. "I'm a Scot, you bloody heathen."

Ali ibn Jehail laughed and turned back, tapping his steed onward, picking up speed.

They were traveling into the hot part of the day. It was madness, pure madness; no matter how important the alliance was, baking their brains out in midday sun in the bleakness of the Arabian desert wasn't worth it. They should have gotten up in the middle of the night, one or two o'clock in the morning, and pushed on then. The animals couldn't take it. The two men couldn't take it. MacLeod was beginning to suspect, however, that Ali ibn Jehail had had all his brains kicked out by a camel; he seemed determined to make the European wilt. They'd been doing it for days now. Ali was not becoming better company on longer acquaintance.

MacLeod was grimly determined that he would *not* wilt. As soon as this errand was done, he was going back to someplace civilized. If Ali wanted to push, fine. It would be over with that much more quickly, and he could go back somewhere where he could get a bloody cold Highland ale.

Thinking of ale made him thirsty. He leaned forward, cautiously—the first time he'd tried this, centuries ago, he'd pitched headfirst over the camel's shoulder—and unhooked a red leather bag from the saddle. It was capped by a leather plug, attached to the bag by a thong.

The water was too warm, and tasted suspicious; he didn't

want to think about how the bag had been cured. But the liquid was wet, at least, and soothing to lips and tongue parched by the unrelenting heat.

There wasn't much left in the bag by the time he finished. Fortunately he had a canteen and two more water bags, filled the night before at the oasis spring. He'd asked how far they had to go before reaching the next watering hole, and then doubled it, considered the source of his information and doubled it again.

What he'd neglected to consider—what he had forgotten, much to his chagrin—was the effect of travel in the midday sun. Even in December, it was hot during the day. Winter merely meant that it was also very cold at night.

Up ahead, Ali was slowing down at the base of a dune, looking up at the sky and around the horizon, picking out landmarks. Duncan guided his own mount up beside the other man's, yanking its head away when it tried to bite. "What is it?" he asked, his hand straying to the butt of the pistol shoved into the belt of his robes.

Ali was staring up once more into the pitiless blue sky. His camel bawled suddenly, nearly startling Duncan into a fall, and circled uneasily.

"What?" Duncan demanded. "A ghibli?"

"No. No ghibli." Ali spared him a glance, then looked up to the sky again. "Vultures."

MacLeod looked up. "I don't see any."

Ali nodded.

"So why is that a bad thing?" Duncan had long since concluded that patience was required in dealing with Ali. "There's nothing dead out here to attract them."

"Aye." But Ali still appeared uneasy. He looked around at the surrounding dunes, chose a spot, and moved his camel over to it. "It is time to rest," he said abruptly. "We will make camp here, sleep during the heat of the day. We go on to the wells of al'Ghazal when the sun goes down."

"Well enough."

The two men slipped down from their camels and set up a dry camp, staking out lengths of black camel hair tenting propped up at one end to provide shade. Whining and grunting, the camels settled, lowering themselves to the ground in three distinct stages, front, back, front, and Duncan set out fodder to occupy them and removed the saddlebags, loaded with gold, to keep at his side. They hit the ground with a distinct thud, and MacLeod thought Ali's head jerked in response to the sound. Not likely, he thought, and settled on the ground in the shade of his own little shelter, leaning back on the saddlebags as if they were pillows. He couldn't disguise the fact that the saddlebags contained something valuable, but he could make it clear enough that the guide would have to go through him to get to it.

"How far to the wells?" MacLeod asked casually.

Ali shrugged. He seemed restless, fidgeting with the cloth, getting up again to bring his water supplies under its shade. When MacLeod repeated the question, he said at last, "God knows."

"I have no doubt," MacLeod said, barely disguising his irritation. "Do you?"

"I am the best guide in all the Nefud," Ali responded indignantly. "All men know that Ali ibn Jehail is the best guide in Arabia."

"Aye," Duncan muttered. "You and yon bloody tick." But he didn't say it loudly. Meanwhile, Ali had checked over his water bottles and taken a long drink. Seeing the other man's disgust, he grinned toothlessly at MacLeod and offered him his second bottle, clearly trying to make peace with his employer.

It was a generous gesture, not to be taken lightly. Nodding, the Immortal took the waterskin and drank deeply. As always, the water had picked up the flavor of the skin and other, more doubtful exposures, but it was liquid and welcome nonetheless. Handing it back, he smiled in response to Ali's grin. "How long will we be here?" he asked.

"Oh, past sundown," Ali assured him. "One cannot travel in the full face of the sun."

MacLeod nodded. He wasn't really hungry, but he got a dried date from his supplies and put it in his mouth for something to suck on as he settled under the cover of the makeshift shelter. Something was wrong, obviously, but Ali would never tell him about it. Meanwhile, he could use the rest, and the blessed relief of shade.

Looking out onto the desert sand, he squinted against the glare. Heat, reflected from white sand and pale rock, shimmered in the air, and he blinked hard. For a moment the whole landscape seemed to swim before his eyes.

The woven camel hair stank in the sun, absorbing the heat. He used his quirt, a stick about four feet long covered with braided leather, to prop it up better in the middle, and prayed for a breeze. Not a big breeze—not the ghibli, the searing wind that carried sheets of sand to scour the flesh from a man's bones—just a little one, to ruffle the stained silk robes, dry the sweat from his hair, make a fish-scale ripple in the surface of the yellow-white sand. A little breeze to comfort the soul and remind a man that there was a life beyond this one, a moment of Paradise; a little breeze . . . he lay back on the sand, feeling a bit dizzy. He needed more water, he thought. Too easy to dry out in the desert, dry and wither and fly away on the wind.

The camel, picketed ten feet away, belched, and its saddle rocked, the red and black tassels swinging. MacLeod muttered, and the camel swiveled its head around to give him a serene, long-lidded look, unconcernedly chewing its cud.

"You spit at me, by God I'll spit back," MacLeod warned the animal. It did not appear impressed. Perhaps he was mumbling too much.

It was too hot to sleep. The layer of sand just beneath the surface was barely cooler; rolling heavily onto his side, ignoring the canteen digging into his ribs, he burrowed into it and prepared to wait. He had forever— *What's the use of that thing, counting minutes when we have forever*—

The shadows stretched long in the other direction when he opened his eyes again. The camel remained in his field of vision, still chewing thoughtfully. He lifted up the quirt and got unsteadily to his feet, brushing the sand away. He staggered, had to catch himself.

There was only one camel. Only one length of camel hair cloth.

"Ali!" The sound of his own voice set his head to pounding.

The words vanished into emptiness, unanswered.

"Ali!"

Ali was gone. So were the pouches of gold MacLeod had been sleeping beside so protectively, and the water bags. The blurring of his vision and the aching of his head told him he should have been more suspicious of his guide's unexpected generosity with the water.

There weren't even any tracks; he was surrounded by high soft dunes, speckled with patches of brush. As he pivoted, cursing, looking for some sign of his erstwhile guide, the breeze he had prayed for hours before whipped up a spume of white sand from their edges, subtly changing their shape even as he watched.

All morning they had moved north and west, deeper into the desert. The Nefud was not the soft sea that much of the Sahara or even the Rub al'Khali was; it was nearly barren ground, with only a few struggling plants in among the rocks—dry, hard ground covered with a thin layer of sand eroded by wind.

Now, with the sun setting, the shadows pointed a counter to his way—the direction opposite his line of travel. The trouble was, a general direction was no help in finding an oasis that was no more than a dot on the map. It would be all too easy to miss.

Ali was gone. MacLeod cursed himself for a fool, and worse than a fool.

The only question was why Ali hadn't bothered to take the second camel as well. Perhaps he intended to say they'd been separated, and MacLeod lost.

Perhaps not; perhaps he'd meant to wait until his victim was dead and then come back for it.

MacLeod shrugged. It raised more questions than it answered, and it really didn't matter.

Without the gold, his mission was probably doomed to failure, but— *Not everything is written—*

—and he was an abominably stubborn Scot. His mission had been, after all, to persuade a sheikh to join Faisal. Not merely to deliver bags of gold.

The effects of the drug were beginning to wear off.

He sighed, gathered up his length of tenting, and marched over to the camel, batting it smartly on the nose as it reached around to nip. He clambered aboard, clinging for dear life as the camel lurched forward, and back, and forward again, groaning loudly.

"Ah well, I've never died of thirst before," he said philosophically, turning to follow the path of the shadows toward their source, the setting sun. "I expect it'll be just as bad as all the other ways."

A camel could go seven to ten days without drinking, MacLeod had heard. But those conversations were in the white marble halls of Cairo, and the shaded seraglio of Constantinople, and within the thick, insulating mud walls of Algiers, cool places where one could conduct a civilized discussion over tea. Now, alone in the middle of the great northern desert, there was no one to talk to about camels save the animal itself.

He traveled as far as he could that first night, carrying a mouthful of water from his one remaining canteen, without swallowing, for what seemed like hours. He let the camel set its own pace, and after a time, its own direction, hoping it would be able to scent water, or other animals, or some kind of life. The rhythm of the camel's large soft pads against the sand, the languid, steady sway, nearly sent him to sleep. He looked up sometimes, orienting himself by the stars, to see which way he was going. It was still, always, north by east.

Around six in the morning the camel came to a stop. The cessation of motion jolted MacLeod to alertness, and he looked around himself wearily. This was the hour of morning prayer, when the meuzzin called over the tents of the Bedouin and the flat rooftops of the cities alike, "God is great; there is no God but God. Come to salvation! Prayer is better than sleep!"

There was no muezzin here. He could hear only the breathing of the camel, the grinding of its teeth, the whisper of the single rein against its neck, and the creaking of the saddle as it moved its head. They were loud sounds in the immanent silence of the deep desert.

Deciding that the man atop its back was overlooking its cue, the camel groaned and knelt, and turned its head again to look slantwise at him. Sometime during the night the tick, gorged to repletion, had fallen off; only a streak of blood in the yellow-white hair remained to mark where it had been. MacLeod squeezed his eyes shut and opened them wide again, stirred himself and slid off, awkwardly.

He had no feed, no water for his animal, and it bothered him. He could only stake the beast out and remove its saddle, hoping he remembered how to put it back on again when the time came. The sun was a quarter over the horizon when he was finished.

Since there was no guide to be appalled by it, he removed his kaffiyeh and robe and let the morning air wash over his body. He debated whether to go through his own version of a morning prayer, and decided that even in the Nefud, with no sign of friend or foe within a hundred miles in any direction, there was something to be said for discipline: so the camel chewed its cud and watched as the man moved through the ritual kata of meditation and battle, turn and twist and leap and strike, the long curved blade of the katana whistling through the air, cut and parry and guard, flowing from one movement into another with the pure mindless focus of years, decades, centuries of mornings, afternoons, evenings of these same movements, of Immortal practicing endlessly to remain so.

The sweat had dried on his body even as he finished the final, formal salute to his imaginary foe, and he put the sword away, resumed the robe, and permitted himself one more mouthful of his meager store of water. The camel didn't appear distressed as yet; it had drunk deep only two days ago. Most likely, he thought, it would last longer than he would. Especially if he kept on exercising.

He got out the length of cloth and propped it up into his makeshift tent once more, taking the precaution of keeping the canteen with him. It would be no more than he deserved to wake and find the camel gone, too, and with it his saddle; at least the water would stay with him.

It was easier to fall asleep this time. He dreamed, as he often did, of death and dying, of the terrible power of Quickenings. He dreamed of Hamza el Kahir.

Remember.

He remembered. He relived, in his dream:

Xavier St. Cloud, a dark figure robed in black, slender, almost Oriental in appearance, leading his friend to a place beyond the walls, where they could settle their challenge without mortal eyes to witness. Hamza, older to the naive eye, his hand on the silver, ringed hilt, striding after, with only the angle of his shoulders to reveal he was not only determined, but afraid. MacLeod had watched from the shelter of the crumbled wall. He could not interfere. It was a Rule.

Hamza had fought bravely and well, showing the same grace and skill and speed MacLeod had admired despite himself in the house in Algiers. He was, as MacLeod had so brashly told him, good. But from the very beginning of the battle, he could see that his mentor, his friend, was not nearly good enough. Xavier had toyed with him and then, finally, taken his head. Heart aching, Duncan had realized how easily St. Cloud would have dispatched him as well. Hamza had known that; it was why he had come back, to die in his place.

When the Quickening erupted, MacLeod had run toward the site of the battle, knowing it was too late. He could only stand at a distance and watch as the surviving fighter took Hamza's power, a display of light and energy nearly invisible in the desert sunlight; and when it was over, St. Cloud had looked up at him and grinned, as a dragon might. He had fallen back a few paces from the malignancy of that grin, and by then St. Cloud had recovered, found his horse, and wheeled away.

Other travelers had found him there, on his knees, weeping unashamed by the headless body, clutching the ornate watch Hamza had entrusted to him. They concluded he had done murder, and he had had to flee into the mountains and desert of North Africa to keep from losing his own head to a judicial execution. It had been a long time—a very long time—before he managed to make his way back to Europe.

The dream kept returning to the image of Hamza's head, staring at him empty-eyed from the sand, speaking to him in the pure language of Granada: *Remember me.*

His friend, his teacher had fought for him. Died for him. Even in his dreams, he could not forget.

Chapter Thirteen

Enclosed please find a comprehensive list of the Immortals identified in the North African/Middle East region. Note that the list is shorter by three than the last census; Enver al'Ghazir lost his head in a criminal execution (a tragedy; he was probably not guilty), thereby ending three and a half centuries of life. Solomon ben Judah has disappeared. No one has sighted him in more than sixty-five years, so with reluctance I conclude that he should be presumed dead. Abdullah Mirza has been found dead in an alley in Baghdad. We do not know for certain who has taken his head.

We have temporarily lost contact with Duncan MacLeod. He has been sent on a mission on behalf of the Arab Bureau. I have alerted our fellow Watchers in the desert; they should be quite pleased to have another Immortal to observe. This one is far more congenial than many are.

——Harrington-Smythe

Something tickled. MacLeod woke up with a grunt, batting at the silk robe bunched up around his body. It was midafternoon, and sweat dripped off his body and pooled in the cracks and crevices. The tickling continued.

The robe was filthy. He could barely distinguish the brown-and-cream embroidery around the collar and slit neck from the rough-woven silk it decorated. Traces of gold thread remained, glinting even in the shade.

A fold of the cloth moved. The tickling sensation moved with it. He inhaled carefully and held his breath.

The fold moved again.

"Ah, bloody hell," he breathed. He lay back, very cautiously, propping his head up to watch the progress of the disturbance across his chest.

He knew what it was: some insect, likely poisonous; with the way his luck had been running lately, it was most probably a scorpion. Some ten minutes or an hour later, his sour guess was confirmed when a straw-colored creature, with a body no bigger than his thumbnail, edged out of his sleeve and onto his bare arm. The segmented tail arched high over its back.

It probably wouldn't kill him, which was a pity in a way. If it stung him and killed him, at least he'd revive, healed. If it stung him without killing him, he'd be miserably sick, at least for a while. He wasn't at all sure he could brush the thing away before its tail jabbed into his flesh.

So he watched as it edged along the pale inside of his right arm, unable or unwilling to navigate the dark hair on the back, stopping and reversing, feeling its way along. It was a bizarre way to pass the time, watching the little messenger of death navigate his skin; it reached the area just above his wrist, where the veins stood out and jumped with his pulse. The skin was slick with sweat, and the little scorpion stopped to sample the wealth of moisture.

Duncan watched, careful not to breathe on the little one as it tested, and moved, and sipped.

Even a scorpion couldn't live on salt sweat. It skittered two inches back up his arm; the tail, with the deadly stinger, bobbed consideringly.

It wasn't as if he could go anywhere, after all. It was still too hot to travel, and there wasn't room to jump up and get away. So he lay there and watched, and wondered if his trip would be delayed that much more, by chance and the sting of a scorpion.

The little feet stepped, and stepped, and stepped, each touch barely there, each one a nearly unbearable sensation. He had nearly made up his mind to crush it and take the chance he'd drive the stinger in himself, just to be rid of the thing, when in an excess of energy it skittered over the cliff-edge of his arm and plopped softly to the sand.

He jerked the arm away, and the scorpion's tail whipped down, barely missing him. The scorpion lifted it again, warningly, and skittered toward him. It would be amusing, almost—such a fierce small insect—if it weren't for its venom. Still, the thing hadn't actually hurt him.

He shoved up a ridge of sand and took the scorpion with it, pushing it into the sunlight, out of the shelter of the little tent. It occurred to him briefly to wonder about the camel, but it wasn't likely a scorpion that small would even notice something the size of a full-grown camel, and the stinger probably wouldn't even reach through the hair to skin. The beast would be all right.

The scorpion, defeated, stalked away.

Duncan sighed and stuck his head out from under the tent, squinting against the glare of the sun. The camel was still there, calmly chewing its cud; presumably it slept at some time or another.

The sun was beginning the slide down the sky, but it would be hours yet before it was cool enough to resume his journey. He reached behind him for the canteen and shook it.

It sloshed, not loudly enough. He estimated perhaps three more mouthfuls before his water was gone. Two more long swallows, and then he'd begin dying in earnest.

Thirst would take him before hunger. Neither was a pleasant way to die—well, he had yet to find a pleasant way. He sighed. He'd live through it; wake only to die again. And again. And again.

Being Immortal wasn't always all it could be.

Shaking out his robe and the cloth of the kaffiyeh, he looked them over for evidence of more many-legged visitors. Sure enough, another scorpion, twice the size of the first, plopped onto the sand and scuttled away, leaving Duncan, shuddering, staring after it. "Have you a nest, then?" he muttered, falling back on the accents of his youth. "Wee wicked beasties . . ."

The camel swiveled its head to look him over. The two regarded each other in silence for some moments. "I suppose," MacLeod remarked ruefully, "it wouldn't be fair to make you go on in this bloody heat."

A response was beneath the camel's awesome dignity.

With a rueful chuckle, Duncan checked the stake and tether, and then looked around for the tallest dune available; but they all seemed the same. Picking one at random, he began the scramble upward.

The sand slid under his feet, and he threw himself forward, catching at the small shrubs that somehow grew there. Little bits of pain dug into his palms and healed almost instantly, only to bite again and again into his skin. His efforts brought him meager results; each foot slid downward in the shifting, slippery surface nearly as much as it forced his body upward.

Finally reaching the top of the dune, he stood and looked around, breathing hard. Before him lay a row of identical cream-colored hills, ridged and wavering like a sharp-backed snake, with the breeze ruffling ribs and scales into their sides. Behind him was the same.

Above him, a flawless sky stretched from horizon to horizon. What was it Ali had been looking for, MacLeod wondered. Clouds? It couldn't be; there were never any clouds here.

There was nothing. Nothing but sky, and sun. He had to narrow his eyes to slits to see the miles of nothing above him. There weren't even any birds; at least he didn't have to worry about vultures plucking out his eyeballs. . . .

No birds.

No water?

That was what Ali had said he had failed to see; the vultures of the desert. Which might or might not mean that the oasis they'd been looking for was much, much farther away than they'd thought. Birds could fly, though. Water couldn't possibly be *that* far. Still, like any living thing, they were more likely to be around water.

More likely Ali had simply decided that leading the European through the desert had lost its amusement value, looked for the appropriate signs of desolation, and abandoned him to die. A wry smile twisted its way across MacLeod's lips. He hoped he'd run into Ali again sometime, if only to see the look on the man's face.

No direction revealed more appeal than another. His original plan, to let the camel choose, still seemed valid. He slid down the side of the dune again and set up his shelter not far from the animal to wait out the remaining hours of sunlight.

He allowed himself half his remaining water, and then saddled the camel and mounted. It bawled protest, tried to bite, then rocked to its feet. Then it simply stood, refusing to move without urging.

"Y'stay here, y'fool, we're both dead," MacLeod explained irritably. "And only one of us will wake from it. Move!" It was beginning to seem perfectly reasonable to talk to an animal this way, for lack of any human dialogue. He'd worry about it, if he hadn't done so on more than one occasion in his life. When the animal failed to reply he whacked it, just hard enough to emphasize the point. The camel submitted, grumbling.

They followed the fold of the dunes, the steady pacing exerting its usual soporific effects. As the sunlight faded, a light breeze sprang up. The sweat of his body evaporated almost immediately, leaving a crust of salt almost as gritty as the sand.

He rested the next day during the heat of the sun, and the next, hoarding the last of the water, watching with grim interest as his body shut down under the relentless sunlight.

By the third night, the folding, shifting dunes led them to the top of one of the ridges, and the camel paused, as if waiting for better directions from its rider. Duncan only sat, looking up at the fathomless sky, a swath of black velvet scattered with chips of diamonds, rubies, emeralds, topazes. He had never seen a sky so dark, stars so clear. It was, he decided, worth dying to see, at least if one was Immortal.

The desert floor was still comfortably warm, even though it was cooling quickly; the temperature would plunge as the night wore on, and he would be glad of the body heat of the animal he rode. He was beginning to feel the effects of dehydration. His tongue was thick and dry. He was blinking more often, trying to focus dry eyes. When he had drunk the last time, he could feel the liquid soaking down inside him all the way to his gut. It wasn't enough. The end was coming.

He had heard, somewhere, that one could sacrifice a camel and get at the reservoir of water that kept them going for days at a time. He wasn't sure it was true, and even if it was, he didn't know how.

The camel was sniffing at the breeze; MacLeod could hear it, feel the animal's lungs heaving beneath him. He could only hope it found something.

After a time the camel moved on again, and MacLeod stopped looking up at the stars in favor of keeping his balance. He debated finishing up what little water he had left, decided he might as well; it wouldn't delay the inevitable by more than an hour or so. His hands were unsteady as he untied the canteen from the saddle and lifted it to his lips.

The last swallow was enough to revive him only momentarily. Hot from the sun, the fluid slipped past his parched tongue, a single trickle escaping out the corner of his mouth. He wiped at it with the back of his hand, sucking at his skin to rescue it, and replaced the cap on the container.

He fumbled, and the canteen fell to the ground. In one stride the camel had left it behind.

There was some reason he should go back, pick the empty canteen up and carry it with him, but he couldn't remember what that might be. By the time he worked out that he'd have to have something to carry water in if he should actually find some, it was far too late to go back. The container was lost.

Meanwhile, the camel swayed on, as if it were being ridden by a competent driver with a specific destination in mind. MacLeod's chin fell to his chest and he closed his eyes. They were very heavy, after all, and it seemed more effort than it was worth to keep them open. The camel was perfectly capable of navigating its own way through the darkness, in the nighttime, by itself—better able than he himself was.

The steady pacing never varied, never slipped or tripped or jarred its passenger. MacLeod was content to let it pick its own pace as well as direction. His chin rested on his chest, and his eyes drifted shut. He was dizzy, sick. Only the balance of centuries of training, and the smoothness of the animal's stride, allowed him to remain perched in the camel saddle.

Somewhere ahead of him—he was almost certain it was ahead of him—was the tribe and the oases of the Rushallah. His hand drifted uncertainly to his side, seeking the keys to the leather pouches that had contained bars of gold. They— needed the alliance—the gold—

Chapter Fourteen

*Three new Watchers have been recruited in North
America. Our one remaining Watcher in the Chinese
Imperial Court has died of a heart attack without
recruiting anyone to take his place. This puts us in an
untenable position with regards to the Immortal
currently identified as living in the Forbidden City.*

*Duncan MacLeod's escort in the deep desert has
been found murdered in the streets of Damascus.
Apparently he robbed and abandoned MacLeod to
the mercies of the desert. He had no way, of course,
of knowing how futile that was. Meanwhile, MacLeod
is alone, somewhere in the northern Arabian
desert . . .*

—Harrington-Smythe

The Turkish headquarters at Azrak were, Aziz Mirza Bey decided, boring. His personal accommodations weren't any
better. The whole town, in fact, was an insult to a man of his
importance.

He moved around his rooms, touching things, as he often
did when he was nervous. He was very nervous, lately.

He had many beautiful things, hidden away in his quarters; paintings from France and Italy, Easter eggs and holy icons from Russia, silk rugs from ancient Persia, copper trays from Damascus, glass from Venice, the latest in rifles from America. Jewels from all over the world. Aziz Bey's father had been a collector, and his father before him, and their son and grandson had continued the tradition.

Their *foster* son and grandson, he corrected himself, and his fingers brushed an Attic vase and snatched themselves away quickly, as if someone would chide them for it. Ten nights ago he had returned to his station in Azrak from Baghdad and the funeral of his father.

Abdullah Mirza had been high in the councils of the ruling Turks. Aziz had met many of his father's friends. He had spent much time going through his father's possessions, choosing the best of them to keep, selecting the things to give as gifts to those who could help his career advance, perhaps even to the Sublime Porte itself.

He had found his father's diary, and in it discovered he was no true son of Abdullah Mirza son of Hassan. He was a foundling, a man without a name at all.

No one in Baghdad seemed to know about his status. His mother had died years before, and he had no siblings. He had gone through the motions at the funeral, shocked with loss and with greater than loss; now he looked at the beautiful things in his home and wondered if he had any right to them.

He shifted the position of a ceramic horse, acquired by Abdullah God knew how from the Forbidden City itself, and gently blew the dust from its back. They were beautiful things, beautiful, and now they were as lost as he was, with no rightful owner to call them his own. He felt guilty about even standing here, in his own treasure room.

He was twenty-seven years old, and he felt as if an anchor line to a past and history he knew and understood had just been severed, leaving him adrift.

His father's friends had counseled him, telling him that he was in shock from the loss of his father—the man had been found beheaded in an alley!—and it was no wonder he was confused. Give it time, they had said. It is the will of Allah; accept it.

And he would, one day, he knew.

But all the things he had accumulated to this time seemed meaningless now, worthless, as if they had been accumulated by someone else, for someone else. They were still beautiful, still rare and precious; they were simply not *his*. Not even the ones he had acquired himself on trips to Paris and Rome; he had shown them with pride and joy to the man he thought was his father, and it was all false now.

Turning his back on the storeroom, he locked the door carefully behind himself and went into his study. Here there were books, some of them as rare and precious as any statue, any jewel—but they were books, and that made them different somehow. Aziz's father had not been much for reading. But they contained tales and legends of wonderful things, and Aziz had searched them out and read them and smiled, sometimes, at the fanciful things described: a great cauldron in which one could put a dead man and bring him to life again, a lyre to keep one safe in the halls of the dead, a sword that would allow its wielder to live forever, a djinni-imprisoning lamp.

He had actually found a lamp rumored to be magical; a battered, tarnished thing, it occupied a little pedestal in the corner of his study. No one would think to steal such a pathetic item. It amused him, sometimes, to take it down and rub its side and wish for the next remarkable addition to his collection. The side of the lamp was bright and thin in one spot, where Allah knew how many disappointed believers had rubbed and rubbed, looking for magic. He kept it in the open to remind himself that not every valuable thing was delightful to the eye; some held virtue solely because men believed in them.

It was not the lamp that held his interest now, however.

Just before his father's death, he had been looking once more through his books of wonders, and he had come across a passage which intrigued him. It was a tale of one of the old cities, built who knew how long ago in the wilds of Syria, south and east of Azrak, by a great lord who had made his living by robbing the caravan routes across the desert. The tribesmen had said the place was haunted, or so the story said.

He rather thought they said so to keep strangers out of their own private treasure house, but perhaps not. The Bedouin were notoriously superstitious, after all. The place might have been long since plundered and empty. But perhaps . . . not.

Among his father's papers, he had discovered another reference to the city. This one too mentioned the great storehouses of treasure taken from the Egyptians, the Israelites, the Persians. His father—the man he had thought was his father—had been interested in the place; more, he had been interested in a particular artifact, a sword, which was rumored to be hidden in the king's tomb. He had actually tried to recover it, twice, but each time had been turned back by the nomads who guarded the way to the city. The very last entry in the diary spoke of the sword:

> *I have found one of the desert tribesmen, Farid al'Zafir by name, who says he knows of the old tales, and for a chance at the treasure, and for gold, he will guide me past his brethren. In exchange I will protect him from the accusations of theft that would most certainly occur if a Bedouin should appear with any item of great value, and will put him in touch with foreign buyers. I have met with*

*him several times, and he appears honest. Tonight I will
pay him half the agreed-upon amount, and tomorrow he
will guide me to Petra. I can hardly believe that this time,
at last, I will have the sword.*

Aziz Bey brushed at his clean-shaven cheek, his neat soft
mustache, and thought about the sword. His father had been
recklessly eager to own the thing. This Bedouin could have
been the one who had killed him—though it didn't seem
likely, on second thought. The offer of entrée to foreign buy-
ers was worth more than gold, particularly in these days of
war and disruption. More likely someone else had attacked
his father. His foster father.

He had read about the weapon in his own books, he knew:
the sword of Hamza el Kahir, which legend said would allow
the man who carried it to live forever. El Kahir himself had
made it, and was said to have lived many men's lifetimes,
but according to the legend, the sword had been wrenched
from his hand by his great enemy, who had used it to cut off
his head, and thus he had been overcome at last.

It was a typically bloodthirsty tale for children, and he did
not, of course, believe in any magical qualities the sword
might possess. But it intrigued him now for a number of reasons: that his father had been interested in it but had never
managed to find it; that the weapon was associated with a beheading; that it was a new thing, one which Aziz Bey might
take as his own.

Petra was not so very far from Azrak. And al'Zafir could
be found again, if he went about it the right way.

It would only cost him a little time to go and see. And if
by chance the sword were there, why then he would have a
thing which had never been presented to the approving eyes
of the man who had called himself his father, and lied. It
would be his, his alone, and in owning it he would have

some strange, confused victory over the man he thought he knew but had never known at all.

Life returned, as it always did, with a rush, flooding back into him with an abruptness and force that shocked his eyes open, forced breath into his lungs. The world snapped back into focus, and every nerve was alert.

He was aware at once that he was not alone.

His jerk into alertness caused the man leaning over him to jump back, to the merriment of the others crowded around. Duncan's gaze flickered across their faces. They were Arab, Bedu of the deep desert. Some were mounted on their camels, with horses tethered at their sides. All carried rifles, with bandoliers of ammunition crisscrossed over their chests, pistols and knives stuck into their belts. Some had swords as well. He drew in another shuddering breath and relaxed—there were no other Immortals present. His head was, for the moment, safe. Probably.

Pistols—his hand moved to his own belt, slapped flat against his hip. The weapon was gone.

He got to his feet, slowly, cautiously, allowing himself to stagger. He was supposed to be dying, after all.

"Water?" The word came out as a croak, mutilating the language. His audience laughed.

"Who are you, and what are you doing here?" said one of the men surrounding him.

"Water?" he repeated. It wasn't all that difficult to pretend. He rubbed his lips with the back of his hand, turned in an unsteady circle. There were at least a hundred of them. Many had roughly bandaged wounds, brown with dried blood. They had the look of recent, and not particularly victorious, battle. Several were severely hurt, being supported by their comrades.

They were staring at him with astonishment.

"I thought he was dead," the first man said, backing toward his mount. He was holding Duncan's pistol in his hand, and looked as if he might be thinking about using it. Duncan turned to him, as if by chance.

"You are as blind as a Turk," one of the others said in disgust. He unhooked a water bottle from his saddle and tossed it to MacLeod, who caught the heavy weight against his chest and nearly lost his footing in the deep sand. He pried out the wooden plug with a trembling hand and raised the leather bottle to his lips.

It was hot, and tasted of suspicious things.

It was liquid.

It was wonderful.

It splashed down his chest, soaking his shirt.

"He's wasting it," one man said critically. "Why give him water, Abbas? He's only going to die anyway."

"He's a dog of a Turk," another man chimed in.

"I'm no bloody Turk," Duncan mumbled from around the lip of the bottle. There was a murmur of surprise when they realized he was actually speaking good Arabic, albeit with European curses.

"Who are you, then?" snapped another man, on a particularly elegant white camel. He was wearing an agal trimmed in gold, and the room the others made for him proclaimed him as a man of considerable importance among them. "You are not one of us!"

Reluctantly, Duncan stopped swallowing. "I'm looking for—for the Sheikh Yusuf ibn Ashraf al'Saqr, of the Rushallah. I have a message for the sheikh. From the Emir Faisal ibn Hussein." He wiped a trickle of liquid from his lips. The waterskin was considerably lighter now, but he still craved the feel of the liquid in his mouth.

A murmur of recognition rose from the assembly.

"You are British?" the man on the white camel demanded. "From Cairo?"

It wasn't the time to dispute the distinction between Scots and British, MacLeod thought, and besides, it had ceased mattering in any real sense about two centuries ago. "I am. My name is Duncan MacLeod." The rest of it, *of the Clan MacLeod*, beat against the inside of his lips. That had ceased mattering too, long ago, but it was still part of him, ingrained in the bone.

"I am Yusuf ibn Ashraf Abdullah al'Saqr, of the Rushallah." The syllables rolled off the lips of the man on the white camel: God will multiply, son of the honorable one, grandson of the servant of God, the falcon. Duncan thought for an instant of identifying himself in return: the dark fighter, son of the ugly man. It probably wouldn't be the prudent thing to sound as if he were mocking them. Too much water was making him light-headed. He suppressed a smile.

"Peace be with you, Yusuf ibn Ashraf al'Saqr," he said, belatedly realizing the assembly was waiting for a formal acknowledgment. "I am in your debt." It was risky to say such a thing—it was likely to be taken literally—but it happened to be true. "Allah has been most gracious to me, to lead you to me." He had, too.

"Peace be with you, stranger. Are you an infidel or a Believer?"

MacLeod shrugged apologetically and drank again. No whisky had ever tasted sweeter than that too-warm, stale water, sliding down his throat and soaking into all the corners of his flesh. He drank steadily, his throat swallowing convulsively, his face turned up to the sunlight, accepting it, glad once again to be alive.

Finishing at last, he lowered the waterskin and took a deep breath, looking up into the faces of his benefactors. "I am—one of the People of the Book, but not of your faith."

"Kill him and let us go on," someone said impatiently. "He is an infidel. He has no place here."

"No," ibn Ashraf answered. "He speaks well, for an infidel, and a European." He gave Duncan a considering look. "What message do you have from Faisal?"

"That is a complex matter, my lord." He stared up at the other man, knowing he could still be abandoned. He would rather not have to go through that particular death again. "Are you, God willing, going to meet him?" The qualifier came to him naturally.

Ibn Ashraf's eyes narrowed. After a moment he decided that the infidel wasn't making fun of his religion. "Perhaps— God willing." He waved his hand at the assembled men, an expansive gesture that brought his mount around in a complaining circle. "These are the men of the Rushallah, the sons of my father's father's father's father. Before God, we owe no allegiance to the family of Hussein. If it pleases us, we may join him. But Hussein is far from the wells of the Rushallah."

"Or if it pleases you, you may join the Turk?" Duncan drank deeply again. The waterskin was nearly empty now. "Have they offered you gifts?"

"All who know the Rushallah offer gifts," ibn Ashraf snorted. "Come with us, infidel, and we will show you the wealth of the Rushallah."

"Thank God," Duncan muttered under his breath, entirely reverent. Acceptance as a guest gave him at least three days and three nights in which to try to convince them to do what needed to be done without the encouragement of gold. His chances were not particularly good, but they were better than they had been a half an hour before, and that was enough to go on with.

Chapter Fifteen

---

*The Immortal Duncan MacLeod has been discovered
abandoned in the desert, and is now a guest of my
lord Yusuf. (It is most fortunate that my lord was not
hawking this day, or I would not have received the
message concerning him, nor known to Watch for his
arrival.) We have prepared a great feast in his honor.
He remains, of course, among the men, but I am old,
and much is overlooked for me.*

—Rebekah bint Miriam Um Ahmed

The extended family of Yusuf ibn Ashraf occupied a temporary camp around a small oasis, a pocket of green around a
spring. Their herds of goats, sheep, camels, and horses were
scattered among the hills, cropping busily at the gray-green
foliage. There was a small grove of date palms and skimpy
patches of grayish grass; row upon row of brown and black
tents, the color of the raw wool from which their material
was spun, splotched the sands, with children chasing lambs
and camel foals between them. Duncan gathered that he had
been discovered as the Rushallah raiding party had returned
from a less than successful sortie against a rival tribe. Ibn
Ashraf was not pleased with the results.

So, of course, on the second day after MacLeod's arrival, he threw a great feast to honor the rescue of the European. There had to be something to celebrate, after all, and MacLeod was as good an excuse as any.

There was music, tambourines and drums and zills, and men danced outside, occasionally firing rifles into the air in sheer excess of spirits, spearing the sky with flashes of light. Duncan, sprawled against a camel saddle for a backrest, couldn't help but compare it to the last time he had been feted in such a style—but ibn Ashraf was no sultan, and the dancers were more graceful than Amanda had been, even if they were the wrong sex. Here, the women stayed discreetly out of the way, not entirely out of sight as they would have in a city, but still unobtrusive.

Perhaps twenty men were gathered around the remains of the meal, a huge dish of rice and hacked-up mutton in a pool of melted sheep butter. Outside, a storyteller was reciting the exploits of a distant ancestor, in a singsong off-key rhythm. In the shadows outside the rolled-up walls of the tent he could see the darker images of the women, veiled against his eyes, as curious about him as he was about them.

He was replete with rice and sheep and dates, soaked in the drinking of gallons and gallons of water, and he was falling asleep again. He'd slept a great deal in the past day and a half. It was, he realized vaguely, the height of rudeness to fall asleep again at a feast in his own honor—or one of the heights, anyway.

The feast was his first meeting with the tribe as a whole. It was a remarkable piece of luck that he had actually been found by the people he'd been looking for. Ali had at least led him in the right direction before abandoning him.

Ibn Ashraf observed his efforts to remain awake with a certain mild amusement, and after a time decided to have mercy on him. "You have been through a terrible ordeal,

Englishman who wears our robes. Perhaps you would like to rest, and we may inquire further of this matter of ibn Faisal when you are ready?"

"If God wills it," MacLeod agreed, in a barely intelligible mumble.

"Sleep then in my own tent, and be at peace."

There was much to be said, MacLeod thought muzzily as he stumbled back into a pile of fleeces in the back of the sheikh's tent, for the simple generosity of a tribal people. The Rushallah might even outdo the MacLeods for pure benevolence.

At least he had *found* the Rushallah, was his last conscious thought. But Lawrence would be so disappointed—and Tweedledee so gratified—if he didn't manage to *convince* them where their future lay—

"What do you mean, you cannot locate this man? Are the police in Baghdad totally inept?" Aziz Mirza knew the answer to that question, of course, but someone had to suffer the consequences of his growing frustration. It might as well be the two soldiers standing at rigid attention in front of his desk.

He sighed and rolled his eyes, allowing himself to slump back in the leather chair as if the weight of the world's incompetence was too much to bear. "I told you the man was Irzed, and within the last month had been in Baghdad. Surely that should be enough for any halfway competent intelligence operatives? Or am I making a wholly unfounded assumption here?"

The two men stared unflinching at the portrait behind him.

"We have located the band," the senior of the two said at last. "They don't seem interested in our questions, sir."

"I am not interested in your problems, Sergeant. I expect you to find the man. I wish to speak to him—speak, mind you, *not* interrogate!—about some of his dealings with my late father."

"Condolences on your loss, sir."

Aziz's lips tightened. "Yes. Thank you, Sergeant. Dismissed."

The two men saluted stiffly, pivoted, and marched out.

Aziz rolled his eyes again. No wonder they couldn't communicate with the desert tribes. But the lack of imagination and style was typical, typical of what he had to deal with every day. He lit a cigarette and exhaled a thick plume of smoke, as if the veil would obscure the more unfortunate aspects of his daily life here.

His office at the little command post in Azrak was far too Spartan for his tastes. His desk was battered wood, scarred with use; the walls were yellowed with years of cigarette smoke and flyspecked to boot. The only touches of luxury—of humanity, in his opinion—were the leather chair, imported from London, and a little seventeenth-century painting on the wall. The landscape provided the necessary balance to the official portrait of Kemal Ataturk which hung, by political necessity, behind the desk itself. He had no fear the little painting would be stolen; the dolts he had to contend with wouldn't have known great art if it had bashed their thick heads in.

The place stank of years of use. It was noisy, too; the office didn't even have its own door, and Aziz sometimes thought the uncertain rattle of the typewriter in the anteroom, coupled with the incessant yammering of the marketplace outside his window, would drive him mad.

It was all too much, really.

But then there was Petra—if he could only find his way in. If there really was treasure there, perhaps he might even bring himself to sell off some of the lesser items in his—foster—father's collection. Then he could afford to resign his commission, perhaps even, once this ridiculous war was over, go live in Paris, where one could find civilized conversation, where people appreciated art and history. He could be the person he really was, deep inside, a cultivated, civilized man—not a petty little bureaucrat in a tiny little outpost in the backwaters of the Turkish empire.

He smiled, exhaling another cloud of smoke.

Yes. Petra held the key.

The call of the muezzin woke MacLeod all too early, a few days later, in the dim gray light of a winter desert dawn. The Rushallah had extended their hospitality indefinitely beyond the traditional three days and nights, and he had spent the time eating and sleeping and resting and getting to know the men of the tribe, remembering the lessons about manners Hamza had taught him so long ago. Fortunately he was a heathen, and not expected to pray at an hour which, in any civilized nation, would be dismissed as ungodly.

Fortunately or otherwise, getting up early for prayer meant breakfast came early as well. All too soon, one of ibn Ashraf's sons came in to shake his shoulder and awaken him. As soon as he opened his eyes the boy went skittering backward, as if expecting him to turn into a demon. When MacLeod laughed, the child fled.

When he finished his morning ablutions, ritual and otherwise, he found ibn Ashraf seated in the fore part of the tent, surrounded by the elders of the tribe. The sheikh indicated the remains of a tray of bread and fruit. Duncan politely indicated he wasn't hungry at all, allowed himself to be convinced, and then ate like a starving man. He had not thought, after the night before, he'd had any room left to be hungry. He'd been wrong about that, too.

They waited politely for him to sate his hunger before launching into a serious discussion of the health of his family, his antecedents, his sons—with much sympathy for his lack thereof—and the families, health, and history of every other man present. Finally, after what seemed an eternity of this, they got back to the issue of Duncan's mission to the Rushallah.

"You have said you are an emissary from the Emir Faisal," one of the greybeards said. "Is Faisal so poor he sends men alone to do his errands?"

Duncan shrugged. "It is not that Faisal is poor," he answered. "He has camels and men to equal the stars in the sky. But he does not wish, as yet, to alert the Turk to his movements. Thus he thought it good to send one man, with a guide."

Faisal would probably have sent at least twenty, in fact, but the British were more conservative by nature. MacLeod did not feel called upon to make the comparison.

"And what of your guide?"

"My guide is accursed," he said grimly. "The son of Iblis robbed me of the gold meant for the Rushallah and left me for dead. But God is merciful and compassionate, and you found me." Too late to save his life, but that was only a technicality, fortunately. He still considered it a blessing that Ali, the dog, had waited until they were actually in Rushallah territory to drug him.

"Gold?" The elders spoke among themselves excitedly.

"Two hundred pounds of it," Duncan affirmed wearily. "I apologize most profoundly."

Ibn Ashraf's eyes narrowed. "Without gold, how can we come to Faisal? We have no gifts for him save our herds."

The elders pursued this line of thought as well, with some of them pointing out that Faisal would be expected to provide largess in return, while Duncan was momentarily lost in admiration for Lawrence's canniness. The giving of gifts was a great mark of status; he had probably calculated that the gold MacLeod carried to the Rushallah would end up right back in the coffers of the Revolt. It was indeed a pity he hadn't been able to obtain a more trustworthy guide.

"The greatest gift you can bring to the lord Faisal is your support, and the fighting men of the Rushallah," he insisted. "All Arabia knows and respects you."

Except, perhaps, the Irzed, who had just successfully beaten off a Rushallah raid; but some things were best left out of the discussion.

The reputation of the Rushallah was then discussed, reviewed, and duly praised, without a trace of modesty in the telling. The tray of dates was taken away, and coffee was served.

"Why should we support the Sherif of Mecca?" one man asked.

"So that your children may live in peace," Duncan replied promptly. "So that you need not guard yourselves and your herds from those who would steal your horses and your women from you. So that all of Arabia may be one single nation, honored in the family of nations as an equal member." It sounded brave, and proper. He rather hoped it was true.

More discussion ensued.

Duncan listened, answered respectfully when the elders asked him questions, and tried to guess which way the decision would go. One faction seemed interested in aligning with the Revolt. Another wanted to hold out and see if the Turks would make them a better offer. No one was interested in coming empty-handed to the Arab army.

The potential for looting Turkish towns was discussed in detail. Duncan sipped at his coffee, a thick, heavily sugared mixture that would have appalled an American or a European, and mentioned an example or two of supply trains derailed. The weight of the discussion appeared to be swinging toward joining Faisal, but the problem of saving face remained unsolved.

The debate had begun at least its third iteration when a shrill, too-familiar sound brought MacLeod to nerve-tingling alertness. He half-rose, and the discussion died away as the participants stared at him, taken aback at his expression. Ibn Ashraf blinked inquisitively. "What is it you seek, Duncan MacLeod?"

"I heard— "

"What?"

"Swords—"

Chapter Sixteen

We Watch . . .

—Rebekah

And he could still hear the sound of metal shrieking against metal—but there was none of the sensation that would tell him another Immortal was nearby, only the sound of clashing swords.

"Is someone fighting?" he asked, getting to his feet and looking past the crowd of men sitting around the great dish. "I hear fighting."

"Ah, the young men." Ibn Ashraf himself spoke with great weariness. He could not, Duncan thought, be more than thirty himself; several of his uncles exchanged wry glances over the endless tapping of camel quirts against the mats that formed the floor of the tent. The tapping kept the air moving. "They duel for honor, for love. What can one do?"

"Stop them, perhaps?" Duncan stepped over the quirts and past the tent poles, out to the open area. Ibn Ashraf and several of his relatives shrugged and got up to follow him. The sound led him beyond the first circle of tents.

There were two of them, young boys, children really, barely old enough to start beards; they were squared off by the picket lines near the skeikh's tent, glaring at each other and spitting insults, while their respective mothers stood in the shadows of the tents and wailed in frustration and fear.

One of them—Duncan paused at the sight of him. He was undersized, reed-thin, holding an old sword up in guard position against his face, his brown eyes intent upon his opponent. The other boy was measurably bigger and talked more, making rude comments about the first's ancestry.

"Ahmed! Tarif!" ibn Ashraf roared. "What are you doing?"

The two boys circled each other, ignoring him.

"They were racing," one of the women called out from the shadows. "Tarif's mare stumbled."

"He did it himself. He stabbed the frog of her hoof," the bigger boy said, never taking his eyes from the other. This, Duncan concluded, must be Ahmed. "The son of a diseased camel hurt his own horse, and he dares accuse me. I'll have his head for it!"

Duncan, looking at the two of them, shuddered as if a goose had walked over his grave—a saying from the Highland completely out of place here, perhaps, but comforting nonetheless. He could not have told how he knew what he knew about one of the two combatants. It was enough that the fight had to be stopped, immediately, before the situation became any worse.

Tarif didn't bother to respond to the accusation; instead he lunged. Ahmed ducked and responded smoothly, and Duncan cursed as Tarif yelped. A line of bright red appeared across the boy's chest, and his guard dropped a crucial few inches.

Ahmed leaped forward to take advantage of the opening, murder in his eyes, only to be brought up short by one hand on the wrist of his sword arm and another at the scruff of his neck, knotted in the nape of his long gown.

The boy spat a stream of curses and twisted wildly, transferring the sword to his free hand and swinging wildly at the man behind him. "Devil! Pig! Spawn of a whore!"

"Insolent pup," Duncan said calmly, letting go of Ahmed's neck long enough to grab the boy's flailing arm. The sword went flying into the sand. "A little young for matters such as this, aren't you?"

"He's a cheat and a liar," Tarif said, trying very hard not to cry. "And *he* hurt my horse." He was standing well out of reach, his sword half-raised.

"Fatherless one! It isn't even your horse, it belongs to Mehdi!"

"Is what he says true?" the sheikh said to Ahmed, stepping between the two, his face suffused with rage. Duncan could feel the boy stop struggling, and loosened his grip. The boy stepped away from him, giving Duncan an evil glare before turning to the sheikh.

Ahmed looked ibn Ashraf in the eye. "Father, he lies."

Duncan took a deep breath. It *would* have to be one of ibn Ashraf's own sons. . . . Around them, the men jostled for position to see, while the women formed another circle, farther back. Voices murmured back and forth, raised sometimes and then hushed again as the speaker realized he or she might be overheard.

Now Ahmed was jerking his robe back into place, glaring up at Duncan as he did so. "How shall this unbeliever lay hands on me?" he challenged, looking to his father for support. "I will kill him for it."

Ibn Ashraf slapped him almost as the words came out of his mouth, knocking him across the small clearing. His turban went flying, partially unwrapping, revealing long braided hair. The gathered observers gasped.

"This man is my guest! You dishonor me and all our family! As for you, Tarif"—he turned to the other boy, who was still standing forlornly a few feet away, the tip of his blade resting now in the dust before him—"do you have witnesses to what you say?"

"I have no witnesses but God, who knows all things," Tarif responded. "And my mare." In the sunlight, his eyes glistened. The line of red across his ragged shirt was broadening.

"How shall we know, then?" ibn Ashraf asked reasonably.

"I am your son!" Ahmed yelled, picking himself up from the dirt and jamming his turban back on his head. "Will you believe that spawn of a dustdevil over me? It isn't even his horse!"

"Ahmed speaks truly: the mare is mine," piped up another man, leaning on a rifle. "Though I gave her to Tarif to ride. If there is an injury to her, it is I who have the claim."

Tarif made a wordless sound of protest, looking at the speaker: Mehdi, Duncan gathered. He looked even smaller as his claim to the horse, too, was denied. It was as if everything he had was being taken from him—everything but the sword he clutched so defiantly. In a society based on family and relationships and extended family, he seemed to have no one to call upon. He didn't bother to glance behind himself at the woman wailing for him.

"He hurt her himself, and he blamed me because he thought he could claim recompense for the value of the horse," Ahmed snapped, brushing himself off again but staying well out of his father's reach.

"You did it because you were jealous," Tarif returned. "She's faster than anything you have. Or she was," he amended, dashing a tear-track from his cheek.

"If there's only one witness for us to question, perhaps we ought to do so," MacLeod interposed, speaking to the sheikh, before the fight could break out anew. "If you are agreeable, let them bring the mare and let us see what they're fighting about."

Ibn Ashraf looked at him sharply, waved his son's protest to silence. "What do you have in mind, English?"

"You can't," Tarif said at the same time. "She's hurt too badly."

"Then we will go to the horse," MacLeod said firmly.

Intrigued, the crowd followed them, in a large unruly mass, toward the horse lines, pursuing the sheikh, MacLeod, and the children. The scraps of conversation MacLeod could catch had to do with the reputation of the two boys, the bloodlines of the horses involved, and much speculation about the madness of the Englishman and what he could possibly be trying to accomplish.

The herds of the Rushallah stretched across one end of the camp. The riding camels were kept mostly separate from the horses. Some of the valuable war mares were tethered near their owners' tents, but many other horses were tied to the long picket lines. MacLeod wasn't particularly surprised when Tarif pushed ahead, leading them past the pastures and cross a small wadi, to a bare area ideal for racing.

There was no racing going on now, in the heat of the noonday sun. There was only a thin mare, dark gray with youth. Her head was up sharply, watching them, her ears nearly touching at the tips in their effort to hear everything; she snorted and turned, clumsily, on three legs. Her forelegs were loosely hobbled together; her right hind was cocked up beneath her, not touching the ground. Blood dripped freely from it, in steady pulses.

Recognizing the animal's distress, the crowd stopped, all except Tarif, who came up to her slowly and steadily, talking to her all the while, soothingly.

She was a small example of a small breed. If she had been in flesh she might have been almost stocky; her legs were more substantial than they looked. Her head was refined and delicate, her neck long and clean. The boy looked taller standing next to her, until the two adults came up to them.

Ahmed hung back, until a gesture from his father commanded him.

"Tell us again what happened," Duncan said, keeping his voice even for the sake of the horse. He looked her over, laid a hand on her neck. It was wet with sweat, and she tossed her head, eyes rolling, but did not offer to snap. "Tarif, you go first." It was possible, he realized, that ibn Ashraf would object to an outsider taking over in such a delicate matter, but he didn't care. Someone had to find the truth, and he felt a thread of protectiveness for Tarif, who had no one to speak for him. MacLeod had known the instant he saw the boy: Tarif would one day be an Immortal too.

Ahmed sneered.

"We have raced before," Tarif said, without preamble. "I always won. This time, Ahmed met me as I went out to her, and he was laughing, and he challenged me to race in the noontime. But as I led her out I saw she was hurt. Ahmed never came to race. When I came back to the tents, looking for Mehdi for help, Ahmed was already boasting he had won."

"Ahmed?" ibn Ashraf turned to his son.

"By God, he lies," the bigger boy said. "We rode here, and the mare tripped over her own feet and went lame. He accused me of hurting her and said he would claim my own horse as justice. He has always tried to take what others have."

"So you did not see him hurt the mare himself, as you said before?" his father inquired, with deceptive mildness.

Ahmed fumbled for a moment, then recovered. "He did so, in that he rode poorly."

"You say the mare tripped. You saw this?" Duncan was

moving along the animal's off side, sliding his hands along withers, back, and hindquarters. The animal flinched as he passed his hand down her off hind, noting the heat in the leg. Tarif, and now his friend Mehdi, stood at the mare's head, holding her and talking to her.

She wasn't happy about the odd-smelling stranger near the source of her pain, and momentarily snorted and pinned her ears as Duncan patted her lightly. The muscles under his hands tensed, and the injured foot came up higher. Hurt or not, he would have to give the lady her due respect or she would kick his lights out, he thought wryly. But she was essentially a sweet-natured beast, and after the one warning, stood still for him, trembling like a wire drawn too tightly.

There was no heat in the upper leg, he noted, only copious amounts of sweat darkening the horse's flank. The heat began around the cannon bone, and the fetlock: increased blood flow to an injury.

"I saw," Ahmed affirmed to his attentive relatives.

"She is lame because she has been hurt," Tarif snapped. "But you were not here to see."

Panicking at the anger in her master's voice, the mare reacted by lashing out, kicking, rearing; she nearly went down when the injured foot refused to take her weight. It took several minutes to calm her.

Finally, Duncan was able to slide one hand back down the trembling animal's leg once more. Ibn Ashraf moved up beside him, the better to see.

Duncan cupped the hoof in his hand. Someone else poured water over the injury, washing the blood away so they could see its extent more clearly; the liquid soaked redly into the sand, disappearing almost immediately. The horse shuddered at its touch, but remained still, as if finally realizing they were its only source of help. In a moment or two the extent of the injury was clear.

The frog of the horse's right hind, the V-shaped tissue in the middle of the foot surrounded by a hard dark hoof, gaped open and bleeding. It was a sharp, deep cut, small. It could not have been made by a rock.

An outraged murmur went up, and the horse tried to jerk away again, stopping only when it came up against one of the men on her other side. Mehdi reached for the injury, long fingers pausing just above it.

"By God," he swore, "this is an abomination. She is crippled, and will have to be destroyed. My lord, I demand justice!"

"Did I not say it?" Ahmed shouted from behind his father. "He has done it, and he should die for it!"

Chapter Seventeen

There is a dispute between the son of my lord Yusuf and Tarif, the foster son of Safiyyah. It is of interest that MacLeod defends Tarif; perhaps he recognizes the child as one of his own kind. I have long hoped as much: we do not have foundlings among our tribes, deep in the desert. It has been long since I had one of our own to Watch; I feared never to add to our chronicles again.

Safiyyah weeps, in fear for her fosterling. If she knew what God has willed for him, her tears would be endless indeed.

—Rebekah

Beside them, Tarif shrieked in disbelief and dove past them to the mare, grabbing her halter. "No!" he screamed. "No, you cannot hurt her!"

Duncan caught at the boy as the mare rose again, lifting the child into the air, screaming as she put weight on the injured foot. The horse staggered and collapsed, legs thrashing frantically. A hoof grazed Duncan's shin, and he grunted in pain as he snatched at Tarif, swinging him out of harm's way and into Mehdi's arms.

The force of the animal's struggle snapped the hobble on her forelegs, and they clawed frantically at the sand as she tried desperately to get her legs under her again. But the injured leg couldn't help her lever her way up; after a few frantic minutes she seemed to realize it, and lay still. Her long neck was stretched on the ground as if in offering; her jaws gaped and her ribs heaved as she panted.

"Ghazal!" Tarif tore himself free and flung himself on the ground beside the horse, hugging her neck, weeping. "You can't hurt her, you can't!"

"This does not look to me like a boy who would hurt his horse," MacLeod observed levelly. The sheikh nodded, his eyes troubled.

"He did it," Ahmed insisted. "He did it!"

"Then how did you know what happened?" MacLeod said.

Ahmed was silenced for a moment, looking confusedly from the animal on the ground to his father, and the rest of the men. "All of you saw," he replied. "He lamed his horse. Mehdi's horse."

"We all saw," MacLeod agreed. "But none of us knew the nature of the injury until now, except you."

"What do you mean? Father, do you permit this infidel to question me?" He was a small defiant figure, this child-prince of the desert, his sword and his pistol stuck bravely in his belt, with gold thread glinting in the agal, the cord holding his headcloth in place. In his posture and in his eyes was invincible arrogance. "He is a Frankish dog. Is this not a matter for the Rushallah?"

"It is a matter for the truth," his father replied. "I would hear more." He nodded to MacLeod. "Speak."

"Your son said the horse had been stabbed in the frog of the hoof," Duncan pointed out. "But we had to clean the wound to see that it was so. Only the one who inflicted the damage could have known its nature before then."

"That is indeed so," he agreed, his face dark with anger. "My son, how did you know?"

"I—I saw him do it." The arrogance was dissolving as he spoke. "I saw it happen! This stranger lies."

"That was not what you told us before," Mehdi snapped. "My lord—"

"*You* are a liar." Ibn Ashraf spoke with finality, addressing the small figure standing before him. "You have damaged another man's property, and attempted to blame another, and claimed his life as the ransom of your lies. You have threatened and insulted a guest in our tents. You are a shame to the tribe of the Rushallah. We turn our faces from you."

"Father!" Ahmed's eyes were wide with shock. The audience murmured in dismay.

"My son would not shame me so."

"*Father?*"

"*You're no son of mine, and you never were,*" the burly Scot said, thrusting the man he had called his son away from him.

"*Father!*" he screamed hoarsely, but it did no good; the man he had called "father" from the day he could form the word fled from him as if he were the Devil incarnate.

He was left lost, abandoned in the middle of the road, staring after him. "I am Duncan MacLeod of the Clan MacLeod," he cried to the empty road, as much to comfort himself as to affirm his own identity. "I am Duncan MacLeod!"

"Father?" The language was different; the wail of terror was the same. Ahmed was only a boy, less than twelve years old. Duncan MacLeod had been a man grown. One was rejected for a deliberate offense against the core of his culture; the other for no cause he had a hope of comprehending. It made no difference. "Father?"

Seeing too much of himself in the boy's eyes, Duncan was

moved to appeal on Ahmed's behalf. He reached for the sheikh's sleeve.

From the other end of the camp, from beyond the grove of date pines, came the sound of a woman screaming. Then another, and another.

With the screaming came gunfire, and shouts and war-cries. The men of the Rushallah turned to see a wave of men on horses pouring through their camp and pastures, waving rifles and swords, driving before them the herds of cattle and sheep that sustained the tribe's life.

"Sons of the devil!" ibn Ashraf spat. "The Irzed!"

For a moment Duncan was completely confused, until he remembered the raid. When ibn Ashraf and his men had discovered him, days ago, they were returning from a raid on the nearby tribe. Apparently the rivals of the Rushallah were prompt in their vengeance. He barely had time to unlimber his pistol before the first line of tribesmen were upon them.

Bawling sheep drove through the assembled men around the fallen horse, knocking Rushallah men sprawling. The camels came behind them, galloping, overtaking. And behind them came Irzed, dozens of them, guns blazing and swords flashing, on the quick gray and bay war mares of the desert.

Only centuries of practice, honing reflexes to nearly inhuman quickness, saved Duncan's neck from a blade slashing out of nowhere. Snatching out his revolver, he dropped and rolled, stopped only by the mare's back, and fired at point-blank range. The gun roared loud in his ears, and its target threw up his arms and collapsed backward.

There was an Immortal among the invaders, he realized with a sudden chill, but the swirl of battle, the smell of blood and frightened animals, the gunfire and yells and sounds of collision, made it impossible to identify one man out of so many. He fired rapidly, quickly exhausting the chamber;

there was no time to reload; he pulled out the katana to defend himself.

Next to him, still clinging to the neck of the mare, was Tarif, talking steadily to his horse.

"You are a drinker of the wind, a gift of God—be still, my most precious one, my jewel, my most brave, heart of my life, lie still, I am with you—"

Ghazal remained quiet and obedient, her breath coming loud through flared nostrils. Duncan touched Tarif's shoulder. "You stay down too, boy."

Tarif ignored him, continuing to murmur to the mare. A camel thundered by, barely missing the recumbent animal. Ghazal's head jerked up, and Tarif's singsong reassurances doubled in intensity.

In the confusion, Duncan could see one man in particular stopping, hauling his mount around. A knot of Rushallah men attacked him from the ground, and the mounted man swept them out of the way as if he barely noticed the inconvenience.

It was the other Immortal. He, like Duncan, had felt the unmistakable sensation that told him another of his own kind was too near, too close. . . . The threat was not one-sided. The boy remained with his horse as MacLeod rose, the dragon-headed katana in his hand.

The other Immortal's horse danced in a circle, veils of white froth hanging from its lips, until it was facing MacLeod. Its rider caught sight of him and recognized his foe at the same instant, and his heels touched his horse's sides. Tassels flying, the war mare launched herself and her rider at MacLeod like a bullet from the barrel of a gun. Her rider raised his sword high, and the blade caught the sunlight and turned it to glowing silver.

But they were not alone on the battlefield—warring men milled between them, swept them apart. MacLeod found himself sparring fiercely with someone else entirely, dispatching his opponent with frantic efficiency. The other man had the grace to look surprised as the katana swept across his belly, his intestines erupting out of the opening in a fountain of white and pink flesh. He screamed as the blood followed, until his head rolled across the sand.

It was a raid, that was all. The Arab tribes had been raiding each other since time immemorial, for camels and horses and sheep, for the wells that gave life, excitement, and glory. From time immemorial men had died for excitement and glory. The man MacLeod killed—who would have killed him—might have been seventeen.

There was no time to brood about the waste of human life. There was only time to fight. He was good at fighting; he'd been doing it far longer than any of these young men in search of glory. He wasn't interested in glory anymore; he was intent upon keeping the swords and rifles away from the boy behind him, and upon locating the other Immortal who was a greater threat to him than any number of mortals, even mortals with swords.

Tarif was still lying on the mare Ghazal's neck, preventing her from even attempting to rise and bolt. He would not leave the animal. There wasn't room, or time, to force him away, though MacLeod could have pulled him up bodily and carried him. He couldn't afford the encumbrance. Glancing around, he tried to spot the horseman again, but there were too many, struggling knots of combatants.

Raids were supposed to be quick and clean, sweeping down, driving away the herds. Sometimes no one died at all. This raid was different; there was revenge in the air.

"Tarif! You've got to get out of here!" A momentary lull allowed Duncan the luxury of glancing behind himself. He could still sense the other Immortal, somewhere close. He was crouching, poised to strike, and his legs were cramping. There had been no time to straighten and stretch.

"I can't," the boy replied. "She can't run—"

MacLeod sighed. He wouldn't have left a loved horse of his own, either, when he was that age. He could only continue fighting, holding his ground against the waves of battle until they passed over him, beyond him.

With the flow of the battle across the camp went the sounds. Man, boy, and horse were left behind as the raiders wheeled to drive through the camp again, taking the wealth of the Rushallah with them.

All around them, bodies of men and animals lay in still dark lumps. Some of them groaned or cried or whimpered. Most were silent.

One horse nearby remained on her feet, her head hanging, her breath coming hard, her legs splayed out to support herself and her rider. Duncan shook himself and rose unsteadily to his full height, rubbing the palms of his hands against his robe, transferring the katana from hand to hand to do so. He never took his eyes off the horseman. The sensation of *another* was very strong.

The horse wavered to a stop ten feet away, lifting its head in defiance of its own exhaustion. Its rider leaned forward on the pommel and grinned at MacLeod with much the same air.

The Scotsman wet his lips and swallowed. "I am Duncan MacLeod of the Clan MacLeod." It seemed right, somehow, in the midst of tribal warfare, to reassert his own tribal affiliation. He assumed a guard position, raising the katana beside his face, keeping himself between the rider and the child. *You cannot die for someone else*, a small voice in the back of his mind scolded him.

You can defend the weak, he snapped back at it, and took a deep, calming breath.

"You are Frankish!" The other Immortal was momentarily taken aback. "What does a Frank do here?" The tribes of Syria and the north had a tendency to identify all Europeans as Frankish, or French. A few of the southerners distinguished the English. None of them had ever heard of Scotland, much to MacLeod's annoyance.

"Fight," MacLeod said, his temper considerably shorter than it had been earlier in the day, when all he had to worry about was the identity of the meat in the morning meal.

From the expression on his face, it was a defensive position the other man had never seen before, and he leaned one arm against the high pommel of his saddle and looked Duncan over curiously.

"I am Farid al'Zafir ibn Muhunnad, and my people are the Irzed," he informed the air, as if in afterthought. "I have lived and died . . ." he paused to count, to remember, "six times. Including tonight."

His robes were slashed and covered with blood, great black splotches, some still tacky where it had not quite dried. Duncan could not control a sympathetic wince, but he kept the sword at guard.

"My . . . kinsmen did not see me fall, this time," al'Zafir went on, in response to Duncan's movement. He still had not produced a sword. His horse's head was beginning to droop again, and his hand was loose and relaxed. "I did not know there were ones like myself among the Franks," he continued. "Are there many?"

Duncan finally lowered his own sword, but remained ready. The other man could be planning to talk him to death, after all. Though he had never heard a word so sharp it would take a head, he had to admit—

"There are some." He shrugged. "Enough. I'm not here to take anyone's head—unless I have to."

Al'Zafir grinned, his teeth very white against his short

beard. "I too have had my fill of war today," he admitted cheerfully. "Though some other day, some other time, it might be a different tale." He looked past Duncan to Tarif, who was finally beginning to get to his feet. As soon as his weight was off Ghazal's neck, the mare fought to get up.

"Ah, a young one," al'Zafir said, whistling through his teeth. "Does he know what God has willed for him?"

"He does not." Duncan had finally lowered the sword. "Do any of us?"

The other Immortal grinned again. "It is all in the hands of God." Sliding off his horse's back, he stepped forward. "You and I are closer kin, perhaps, than either of us to the tribes we claim. I give thee peace this day, Frank."

"And to you." Duncan was still wary, but inclined to trust the other man. Transferring the katana to his other hand, he took the proffered arm, wondering whether it would be accompanied by a knife in the belly.

Apparently al'Zafir was wondering too, because he stepped back quickly, to a distance more common to Europeans or Americans than to Middle Eastern cultures. His eyes lit on the katana, though, and he held out an impulsive hand.

"What a sword! It is a weapon an angel would carry. Or a demon. Is it permitted—" He broke off with a laugh. "Of course not. Forgive me. I have a passion for such things. I cannot see a sword without yearning to own it."

Duncan smiled wryly. "It comes with the territory." It wasn't a sentiment that translated well; he had to say it in English. Al'Zafir looked confused, then brightened.

"Do many of my cousins among the Franks carry such weapons, then?" he asked, still cat-curious. Duncan moved with him, still keeping himself between the newcomer and Tarif. "I have many, but have never seen one like that before."

"It comes from Japan, a place far to the east, where they make great swords."

"You have been to this Japan? You have seen them?"

"I have."

"They cannot be so fine as our weapons were once. I have some so fine they would cut a scarf of silk—"

"—so strong they would cut a bar of iron. Yes, I know." The katana would do as much, but he saw no need to tell the Bedouin that.

"I would trade weapons with you, Duncan MacLeod. I have an excellent scimitar, of good Damascus steel. But I have never seen one such as that."

He was shaking his head even as the other man finished speaking. "I'm sorry, but no. This is"—he hesitated, searching for the right word—"a legacy from a friend and teacher. I do not have the right to give it away."

"Ah." Al'Zafir nodded understanding. "There are such weapons."

The sounds of struggle from the other side of camp had ceased entirely. The Immortal grinned again, and MacLeod found himself grinning back. "It was a great battle, was it not?" the Arab said cheerfully.

MacLeod's grin faded fractionally as he remembered too many "great battles." The only characteristic they had in common were the numbers of their dead. "I suppose it was."

"You must be very old," al'Zafir said critically, "if the music of the swords no longer makes your heart sing. It would be a great thing to take your head, Duncan MacLeod. Perhaps I will be the one to do it."

"And perhaps I'll take yours." Duncan lifted the katana a meaningful fraction of an inch.

The other laughed. "I give you my word, Frank, when I come for your head, I will do so with a sword worthy of it— worthy to do battle with your own. I know where to find such a thing, in the rose-red city." He swung up to the back of his war mare in a single smooth movement, and pivoted with her. "I only came for the battle," he added over his shoulder. "But I will come again for you. It is written, my Frankish friend."

"I'll be waiting for you," MacLeod yelled after him, as the little mare found strength to leap up the bank of the wadi and away, following after the rest of the vanished Irzed raiders. He could hear the ghostly sound of her hooves against the sand long after he lost sight of her.

Duncan let go a deep breath he hadn't known he was holding as the awareness of *another* faded. The tip of the katana drooped until it nudged a tiny valley in the dust at his feet.

"Who was he? What did he want? Did you know him?" Behind him, Tarif babbled, as if released from a spell. "You spoke as if you knew each other."

"I never met him before this day, I swear," Duncan said wearily, turning to the boy and the horse. "But I knew what he wanted, yes."

"What was it? What were you talking about? Why was he talking about the red city? He is Irzed. He has no rights in Petra. He spoke to you as if you were friends."

Duncan sighed. "No, not friends. Not enemies, exactly, either, though— You'll understand one day. But not too soon, I hope," he added under his breath, staring across the devastation.

Tarif was not—yet—Immortal. But he would be. Duncan knew, without knowing how he knew: one day Tarif would die, and some time after that his eyes would snap open and he would gasp, his lungs shocked that they were taking air once more. Past that point he would never age.

He was too young for that first death. Duncan had seen what happened to children who became Immortal: he had lost one only half a century before, too recently to bear contemplating the loss of another. He looked up and met Tarif's anxious eyes, held out one hand.

"Come with me," he said.

"Where are we going?" Tarif asked, reasonably. "There's nothing left."

"We're going to go back to camp, and see what's left," Duncan said. "And tomorrow, when things are better, we'll decide what to do next."

"I won't leave Ghazal," the boy warned.

Duncan sighed. "I didn't think so."

Chapter Eighteen

==

The women are wailing in the black tents for their husbands, for their sons, for their fathers. There is great sorrow in the tents of the Rushallah. God has willed that many, many have died.

But the Immortal lives on. It is the will of the Compassionate, and we submit.

—Rebekah

MacLeod had no doubt al'Zafir intended to keep his promise about coming back. He wanted the katana, and would consider Duncan's head a more than acceptable bonus. Whether he would take the boy was an open question.

Duncan found himself liking the other man, but he had no idea if al'Zafir was capable of killing the boy in order to take his head, and his Quickening, while he was too new to know how to fight back. There were Immortals who would do such a thing, reprehensible as it was, justifying it as eliminating rivals early. It was nothing but murder, in MacLeod's eyes.

He sighed. After the devastation of this raid, the alliance of the Rushallah might not be of such value to Faisal anymore. On the other hand, this was only one Rushallah band, albeit the primary one, and they had the advantage of numerous other ties to northern tribes. His task wasn't finished yet.

Ghazal, limping badly, followed Tarif like a giant, gray dog back to the main encampment. Early in the morning it had been a relatively neat, pleasant place, each tent with its favorite animals picketed outside, a firepit ready for baking bread, children laughing and running. Now it was silent and shocked, and the trails of smoke that distorted the air stank of burning wool from the tents themselves.

Here and there men and women wandered, picking things up and putting them down again, looking around as if they had been suddenly plucked up by a whirlwind and put down again in a place totally unfamiliar. In places, women wailed and tore their clothing and threw dust on their heads, mourning over the still bodies—smaller somehow in death than in life—of their husbands, fathers, children, sisters. Above the camp, birds circled lazily, as if taking their time at a buffet.

Some of the tents out of the direct path of the livestock stampede were still standing, though poles were knocked askew. Duncan led boy and horse back to the tent of ibn Ashraf to find only the females of the family, directed by a wiry woman of indeterminate years in the process of cleaning up. She was unveiled, perhaps because she thought herself too old for it to matter anymore; she had the leathery, wrinkled skin of someone who had faced the elements too long, and her tribal tattoos were faded and almost indistinguishable. She wore a small fortune in coins—her dowry, her personal property—draped about her neck and arms and hips, over her robes, so that her walk was made music with the soft metallic chiming. She looked MacLeod and the boy over with suspicion.

"What is it that you want?" she asked directly. "Ibn Ashraf is not here; he is with his people."

"The boy needs a place to stay," he told her. "Where is his family?"

Looking over Duncan's shoulder, she shrugged. "His foster mother would have the care of him, but those dogs, spawn of the devil, killed her."

He closed his eyes briefly at the soft, stifled cry that came from the boy.

"Are you taking him?" she asked Duncan directly. In the light of the late-afternoon sun, she had the piercing, dark eyes of a bird of prey, and Duncan felt that he was being measured, challenged in some way. "He has no mother and no father. Will you adopt him?"

"I cannot," he said honestly. He couldn't think of anything else to say. There had to be some other response, but it was just out of his reach; he was desperately tired. He had a feeling this woman wouldn't accept the only excuse he could offer: "I am a soldier."

"He needs someone to watch over him," the woman snapped. "Why will you not do it?" Around her, children and women herded together half a dozen goats, creating a makeshift pen to keep them together. Tarif observed the debate on his future silently, his knuckles white on his horse's lead rope.

"Because I am pledged to serve, and where I travel, there is no room for a child." He took the boy by the hand and led him into the shade of the overhang. The mare followed, snuffling at the scent of burned fabric.

The woman looked the two of them over. "You," she said, pointing at Tarif. "Leave the horse here, and go with Sarsour to find what has been left to us." Observing the anxiety with which he looked at the horse, she added, "I will care for her myself; go."

Reassured, Tarif went racing off after the other children, who were making a game out of finding the greatest number of strayed and panicked animals left to the tribe. The woman watched him go, her lips tight with what might have been anger. Duncan sat, heavily, more tired than he thought.

Once the boy was gone, the woman squatted down beside MacLeod, resting comfortably on her heels. "His foster mother was killed in the fighting, may Allah give her peace. He too will die very young if you do nothing."

He would, in fact; she spoke more truth than she could possibly know. "Why don't *you* take him?" he said, more sharply than he intended.

For a moment she was speechless, and then she laughed, revealing gaps where teeth had been. "I am only a woman," she informed him, as if he had missed the fact. "Tarif is a boy, old enough for the men's side of the tent. My lord Yusuf will not take him, not after the fight with that fool of a son God has cursed me with. Tarif needs a man to teach him the ways of men. It would be well for him if you were the one to do so."

Duncan let go an exasperated sigh. "Perhaps," he conceded. Perhaps he ought to, at least until he could find someone else willing to take on the responsibility. Surely, somewhere in this desert, there was someone who would care for a child. "But I am still a soldier. And I have a duty to perform. There must be some other way."

The woman, evidently by her authority and poise the first wife in the tent of Yusuf ibn Ashraf, nodded thoughtfully. She must be, MacLeod thought, much younger than she looked, especially if she was Ahmed's mother. The desert aged people quickly. "We cannot have him here," she said, sounding regretful. "He has no kin. You could take him to the holy city—to Al-Madinah—"

"It is forbidden," Duncan interrupted instantly. "I am not of your faith."

She nodded again, and brushed idly at the sand before her.

"I thought perhaps you were a Believer; I have heard of some English who are. You know so many of our customs." Her fingers were long, the joints reddened and swelling; they had to hurt, but she gave no sign. "There are those who might care for him, in al'Jawf. His foster mother had kin there."

"I tell you," Duncan repeated impatiently, "I cannot take him. I came to persuade Yusuf ibn Ashraf to join Faisal's army. And then I must go back to Cairo."

"Yusuf ibn Ashraf cannot join anyone's army now," said a weary voice from behind them.

The woman looked up, rose quickly, and stepped back at the sight of her husband. Ibn Ashraf looked at her and sighed. "Go, Um Ahmed. They need you elsewhere. We will speak later."

She jerked her head in acknowledgment and, without so much as another glance at MacLeod, was gone.

Ibn Ashraf settled beside MacLeod and pinched the bridge of his nose. "By the time the sun sets," he said wearily, "she will have counted every living thing left to us, and its condition, and she will know to the last grain of rice how our supplies stand. She is a fearsome woman, that one."

"I'm grateful to you for rescuing me from her," Duncan agreed. "She was about to give me the fostering of the boy Tarif."

"Be grateful she did not decide you needed a wife to care for him as well, for if she had, you would be married by nightfall." He tapped his fingertips to his lips. "Let no demon hear it!"

"Ah, there I'm safe. Surely she would not marry one of your people to an unbeliever?"

"What makes you think you would be permitted to continue in such a miserable state?" Ibn Ashraf was beginning to revive, a little, with the quiet joking, but his face had lines that had not been present earlier in the day. "My friend, it seems that Allah wills your mission will be a failure; it would take the very vaults of Petra to restore our fortunes after this day.

"And besides, before any Rushallah takes horse to ride to pledge allegiance to the Sherif of Mecca and his son Faisal, we have a matter to settle with the Irzed. They cannot be permitted to do this without fear of retaliation. I have sent riders to my cousins of the Howeitat and to the Geysli, and we will wipe them from the face of the desert."

Duncan groaned. It was beginning to sound very much like a desert version of the larger war, with interlocking alliances drawing in one tribe or nation after another—or the more intimately familiar feuds of the Highland tribes. "Are not the Irzed similarly allied? Won't their allies come to *their* aid?"

Ibn Ashraf shrugged. "If it is so written." But he was watching MacLeod's face, listening to him.

"Don't you see, that's the whole point to what Hussein is doing. If you and the Irzed draw in all your allies so that all of the north is at each other's throats, the only ones to win will be the Turks. You'll exhaust yourselves fighting each other, and they'll pick your bones."

There was a long silence, as ibn Ashraf considered. "What would you have me do? I cannot let my honor be stained."

"Join Hussein," MacLeod said intensely. "Help him throw the Turks out of your lands. Serve him well, and then let him seek justice for you."

"There will be better booty when you are a part of an army, taking the treasures of the Turks, than trying to make a meal from the meager bones of the Irzed. Half their animals were yours in the first place—where's the profit in that?" It was an argument that had worked three hundred years ago, with some cousins of his in a similar dilemma. He wondered if it would work here and now as well. Surely the Arabs, also a tribal people, were as pragmatic in their way as the Scots.

"Perhaps it is so," ibn Ashraf said softly. "But I would not come to the tents of a great prince as a beggar, and I have nothing left to give him. Look at my people." He indicated the slowly consolidating herds of animals, the tentpoles being reset, the bodies being lined up on the sand. "They took what gold we had. Most of our horses and camels are gone. What else can I do, but go to my cousins and ask for their help in taking back what is ours?"

"Perhaps you could make a withdrawal from those vaults," Duncan muttered. The vaults must be a local legend; the Immortal al'Zarif had mentioned them too.

But ibn Ashraf was staring at him, a sudden strange light in his eye. "The vaults at Petra are said to be filled with many strange and wonderful things," he said. "Many of them would be gifts fit for a prince."

"Eh?" MacLeod looked up, momentarily confused. He had heard Petra mentioned in connection with archaeological digs; this "vaults" business he had taken to be a metaphor. The local tribes were generally hostile to visitors, and he had never heard of any treasures associated with the place. But ibn Ashraf was speaking as if they were real, with real contents.

"My people do not go to that place," the sheikh was saying, becoming more and more interested in the idea. "It is accursed, and guarded by djinn. The treasure lies there still, waiting to delight the eye."

MacLeod laughed. "Any vaults that might be in Petra have probably lain empty for centuries," he said dismissively. "Grave robbers would have emptied them long since."

"No," the other man said. His face was only inches from MacLeod's, so close they could smell each other's breath. "It is not so. The tribes have guarded the way to Petra for a thousand thousand years."

The local tribes, it suddenly occurred to MacLeod, were the Rushallah and the Irzed.

Duncan arched his eyebrows. "That long?"

On the one hand, Arabic was a language designed for hyperbole. On the other, ibn Ashraf seemed positive that the vaults, whatever they were, were intact. So did al'Zafir, a thought which gave MacLeod pause.

On the third hand, the location of the ancient city was well known to students of Middle Eastern history, so the claim that the way was guarded was doubtful—

MacLeod was beginning to feel rather like an octopus. "What sorts of things are in these vaults you speak of?" he asked, expecting the usual catalog of gold, jewels, magic lanterns—

"The golden idols of the pagan kings of Persia," ibn Ashraf replied promptly. "Also the seven crowns of the lord of Petra, before the djinn destroyed the city. The musical instruments played by the Crusader lords. The Moon of Delight, a great stone set in silver, is also said to be there."

The Scot's eyebrows hiked even higher. Ibn Ashraf was being awfully specific about what had to be a legendary treasure trove. The legends must be very popular around the tribal fires; no wonder al'Zafir had invoked it too. "Could it be, perhaps, that when ibn Ashraf was a young man, he decided to brave the wrath of the djinn and see for himself?" he inquired, hiding a smile.

Ibn Ashraf had no such constraints. His lips softened reminiscently. "Not I," he admitted. "I have been no farther than the entrance to the city. But I had the tale from my father, who went inside the great temple.

"But he was captured by the djinn and thrown from a cliff,

and walked lame ever after. He was permitted to live, he said, because he had not touched anything."

"But an infidel might go in, defy these powerful djinn, and survive?" MacLeod asked dryly, not believing a word of it. "I'm surprised the English didn't strip the place."

"We do not permit," was the simple answer.

MacLeod was beginning to see a pattern forming. He was not surprised to see a smile break out on ibn Ashraf's face, as if a wonderful idea had just occurred to him.

"We could permit *you* to go," he said. "You could enter safely, and take, perhaps, one thing. The moonstone, perhaps, or one of the crowns. That would be a sufficient gift to present to the lord Faisal. We could enter his army with honor, and then call upon his aid to destroy the Irzed. It is a good plan, MacLeod!"

"Is it." He wondered how much of the "good plan" had to do with saving face for the Rushallah, and how much with getting an inconvenient British witness out of the way of a Rushallah counter-raid without actually breaking the tradition of protecting an honored guest.

"Does the lord Faisal wish the allegiance of the Rushallah, or not?"

Remembering the intensity in the blue eyes of the British captain in the Arab robes, Duncan conceded, "Yes, he does." He smiled again. "And while I'm there, perhaps, I should pick up some small trinket for the coffers of the Rushallah, just to help them get back on their feet again?"

Ibn Ashraf affected surprise, as if the thought had never crossed his mind. Behind the two of them, wry laughter indicated that the woman wasn't fooled either.

"Be silent, Um Ahmed," ibn Ashraf commanded absently. This was greeted by a snort of derision, but she moved off to organize some of the women in the preparation of a community meal.

"I have not seen Ahmed," Duncan realized suddenly. "He was not—"

"He lives." The expression which crossed the sheikh's face spoke of his relief. Then it hardened. "But he has still offered you a great insult, and I have said what I have said. It is done."

Duncan raised one hand, unwilling to listen to the words of condemnation, either in fact or in memory, again. "Let me make a bargain with you, ibn Ashraf. If I go, for the honor of the Rushallah, to the vaults of Petra, and retrieve whatever I may find there, will you then take back your son?"

There was a surprised silence. Ibn Ashraf looked at him, his eyes brightening, perhaps with tears, and a smile spread across his face as he took the offered solution to his dilemma. "Is this then the boon you seek in return for doing this thing for my people? If you will do this thing, MacLeod, then I will do as you say, I swear it by the beard of Mohammed, blessed be he."

"And if I find nothing at all, you will still take him back?" Duncan added, seeking to cover all contingencies.

"If you return with no more than a handful of dust and the tale to tell, I swear it," the other affirmed. "May it be written so by the angels."

Duncan let go a breath he didn't know he'd been holding. "Very well then. Now there is the small matter of a guide."

"Why, that is no matter at all," ibn Ashraf said triumphantly, dusting his hands. "Petra is not far from here. The boy Tarif will be your guide. It is a most excellent plan. Give me five days, no more, to persuade the elders, and you shall go to Petra."

Chapter Nineteen

*MacLeod has been persuaded to take the child Tarif
with him to Petra to seek the treasures of the city. In
doing so he has given my lord sufficient reason to
forgive Ahmed ibn Yusuf for his stupidity. May Allah
bless him forever and ever, and may he live long.*
                                                    —Rebekah

On the appointed day, at the hour when a white hair could be
distinguished from a black one, the call to prayer echoed
across the desert, and the soft murmur of submission to the
will of God echoed from outside every remaining tent. The
bodies of the fallen, having been ritually washed the night
before, were buried without weeping; the time of mourning
was over, what was written was written, and it was the will
of God. Duncan watched as the corpses, wrapped in clean
robes, were lowered into hastily prepared graves and covered
with rocks and sand. There would be no markers. No one of
their tribe or family would ever seek this place out. They
were gone, and that was that. They would be remembered in
songs and stories told within the black tents, and that was all.

It was a better memorial than some Duncan had seen.

The few remaining animals were fed and watered in

preparation for travel later in the day. The mother of Ahmed consulted with the other women, and eventually came back to the tent leading a camel, the best of those remaining to them, and Tarif. The animal was burdened with sacks of food and water. She turned it over to her husband and then stood back, watching, as he in turn presented it to MacLeod.

"You will take this camel," he said abruptly. "The boy knows the way; the next wells are not so far." He thrust the leading rein into the Immortal's hand and wrapped his fingers around it with a firm grasp. "The boy will be a blessing to you."

"I thank you," Duncan answered, overwhelmed at the extent of the supplies provided from the ruined tents. "You are very generous."

"We are Rushallah the people of the desert," she spoke up, correcting him, but he could tell that she was pleased. "May God bless you, and your children, and your children's children—"

A shadow crossed her face, and MacLeod wondered how many of those children she had buried that day. She pushed the child Tarif forward, unable to say more.

"And you also," MacLeod responded. He wanted to offer words of comfort, but that was the place of her husband. Ibn Ashraf was a fortunate man.

The sheikh spoke to the boy. "The horse, Ghazal, will be well. We will take good care of her for you to honor Mehdi, who fought bravely for us. You know the way. Do us honor."

The child nodded.

"And you, MacLeod—care for him."

He could do nothing, say nothing, but touch his heart and his lips and his forehead in salute.

"God be with you, Duncan MacLeod. And if it be His will, may you have long life."

"God be with you both, son of Ashraf, mother of Ahmed.

And may you also have long life, and more joy than this day past has brought you."

Um Ahmed looked sharply at him again, and this time she lifted the corner of her headscarf to cover the lower part of her face, as if he had somehow become a stranger, one before whom even an old woman should not show her face. "Go. And may there always be those to watch over you."

So he found himself, as the sun rose in the winter sky, riding a camel again northward, with a small boy clinging behind him. The Rushallah were gone, vanished as if they had never been, and he was caught again in the middle of a vast sea of nothingness. This time, at least, there was plenty of water.

"Where did you find your sword?" he asked idly. Tarif had said nothing so far, accepting the decision that he should abandon the only people he had ever known to go with a stranger with remarkable equanimity. He had been concerned only for his horse and his scimitar. Once assured that he could keep them both—Mehdi was dead, and his heirs weren't interested in a horse that would probably have to be destroyed anyway—he was content.

"It is mine," the boy muttered.

"It's a good sword," Duncan went on. "You handle it well. Has someone been teaching you?"

"It's mine," Tarif repeated.

"All right, then, it's yours." The camel would be a more responsive conversationalist. They kept on in silence as the camel rolled through the miles, watching as the landscape changed from sand to solid, yellow earth dotted with rocks and brush. The camel moved steadily, like an automaton, not appearing to notice the burden it carried.

"MacLeod?" Tarif asked at last.

"Yes?"

"Where you come from, do they ride camels?"

He laughed. "No. We ride horses, or drive in cars."

There was a pause while the boy digested this information. "Horses like ours?"

"No, not like yours. Ours are bigger. Slower."

"Ah."

More thoughtfulness.

"MacLeod?"

"Yes?"

"Do they have sheep, where you come from?"

Aziz Bey consulted his map again, and swore. By the map, Petra had not been very far at all; the map gave no hint of the bewildering jumble of mountains, the barrenness, the desolation. He peered up at the horizon and promised himself that his next purchase, the Law notwithstanding, would be a case of the very best champagne.

He would *earn* this bloody sword.

His men had finally located the guide, two days ago, and Aziz had persuaded him with gold and the promise of a ride in his motorcar to show him the way to Petra, past the guardian Rushallah. The man had assured him that the Rushallah would be no threat at all.

They had set out at first light, even though Aziz was sure the Bedouin was laughing at him for his eagerness. He had tried to awe the man with tales of the treasures; apparently it had worked. The Bedouin had become very quiet and thoughtful.

Now they were stuck in the mountains.

The motorcar had to be abandoned here; there was nothing remotely resembling a road going into the mountains. Even the goat tracks were only a couple of inches wide. "You are certain you know the way into this place?" he asked his guide, who was lounging unconcernedly against a date palm.

"Oh, most assuredly," Farid al'Zafir ibn Muhunnad answered with a grin. "Come, my lord. Follow me."

"Have you had your sword long?" MacLeod asked, as they made their sundown camp. Tarif had prayed and was now eating dried-mutton stew and dates with all the enthusiasm of a very hungry ten-year-old boy. It was MacLeod's turn to interrogate the child for a change.

"Always," he mumbled, through a full mouth.

"Ah." Duncan leaned back against the camel saddle, sipped gratefully at a leather cup of water, and shook his head. "Do you know its history?"

They were into mountains now, and there was plenty of forage for the camel. Their fire was built of dried camel dung, left by previous wayfarers. Tarif was sitting cross-legged on the opposite side of the small campfire, the sword lying sheathed across his knees as he stuffed himself.

"No," he said reluctantly. "Do they have swords, where you come from?"

Duncan sipped again, studying the child over the rim of his cup. He wondered if it would do any good to tell him what he was, what he might become. Remembering himself at that age, he doubted it.

When he came back from Petra, he was going to have to be firm with ibn Ashraf about the child. He had no intention of adopting the boy. The tribal imam might take him. . . . It was a deed of great merit to care for the orphaned, after all. Or was that Buddhism? Occasionally, he admitted, he got the ethical systems confused.

"I know a story about a sword," Duncan said idly, changing the subject. "Would you like to hear it?"

"Yes!"

Duncan hid a smile. Tarif's eyes were very wide—he was trying to stay awake. And like many young boys of his age, he was looking for an excuse. A bedtime story, preferably a bloody one, was as good as any.

"It belonged, a long time ago, to a good man named Hamza el Kahir—a very good man. He made the sword with his own hands. It looked very plain, did this sword; it had no jewels, and its hilt was silver, with a silver ring. But it was the very best silver, made strong. And along the blade ran the inscription—"

"The Daughter of Justice, the Taker of Heads, Drinker of the Blood of Infidels, the Giver of Mercy," Tarif said, nodding his head emphatically. "I know that sword. It is in Petra too."

In Petra? Impossible. It was, MacLeod thought, a wonderful thing how people turned into legends. This place they were going to had obviously become the repository for every wonderful thing that had ever been dreamed of. Hamza would have been amused.

MacLeod kept his voice soft, his words singsong, coaxing the child into sleep as he told him a totally fabricated tale of Hamza and his magical sword, and after a time he was rewarded by seeing the child's head fall forward. Rising cat-quiet to his feet, he crossed the intervening space. He set the weapon aside, carefully, and moved the boy to the robe laid out for him. They would be travelling again in a few hours, when the sky began to lighten. Tarif was a growing boy. He needed as much rest as he could get.

He settled down himself, waiting for sleep to come. He could hear the sounds of the camel, nosing at the scraps of grass and scrub; the sound of the boy's breathing, and his own; the wind, brushing softly against the sand, the scrub, the desert. The sky was black velvet spangled with stars, and for some reason it reminded him of Terezia. He hadn't thought of her for centuries; it must have been the mention of the sword, and Hamza, that made him think of her. For just a moment he could see her face, her lovely sparkling eyes, so clearly in the night that he almost reached out to touch her cheek.

But Terezia d'Alessandro had been dust for centuries. So had Hamza el Kahir, and there was nothing to distinguish between them anymore.

He sighed. Memories of the past weren't getting him anywhere.

He wasn't making much progress in the here and now either, he thought wryly. He was still lost—saving the guidance of a small boy—still looking for what might be a mythical treasure, so a petty princeling could make an appropriate gift to participate in a minor revolt. . . . Well, perhaps not minor from the perspective of the participants, but in the greater scheme of things . . .

The greater scheme of things, and its implications for world history, was more than enough to put him to sleep.

With morning came wind, a wind with mass and shape and color. It boiled on the horizon, brown and heavy, and Tarif pointed at it and shouted in Duncan's ear.

He had already seen. The boy ran to the camel, talking her down, and Duncan assisted. They could use the beast as shelter.

As sandstorms went, it was a minor example, lasting only an hour or so. Humans and animal alike turned their backs to the wind and the stinging sand, knowing there was nothing they could do but endure. Meanwhile, the sand sifted in everywhere, into cloth and tack and ears and eyelashes. Duncan ducked down beside the animal and cursed Lawrence and the Revolt and the Rushallah. He didn't dare look up for Tarif; opening one's eyes into that wind was a guarantee of blinding. The fold of his kaffiyeh, pulled over his mouth and nose, could not prevent the little stinging particles from penetrating.

The camel, finally, announced the little storm's passing, by groaning loudly and heaving itself back to its feet, the sand sheeting off of its sides.

Duncan scratched vigorously at his head, shook sand out of his ears, and batted at his robes. The camel shook itself, yawned, and surveyed the changed landscape with aristocratic disdain. Tarif ran to the animal and stretched up for the lead line.

"The tether is broken," he announced. "There is rope in the pouches. You can fix it—I will go and see our way."

Duncan closed his eyes in exasperation. He was not accustomed to circumstances so utterly out of his control. He would never have the acceptance of circumstances of his rowing-mates, the Jew and the Sardinian of so long ago, to accept what could not be changed. This must be what Hamza had tried to tell him, so long ago, about submission to the will of God.

With all due respect for Hamza and his boundless faith, God in the desert was too capricious for any self-respecting Scot. Duncan wiped the caked sand from his mouth and gave up. "Certainly," he muttered. "I'll repair camel tack and you go exploring. You'll be sorrier than you know if you break your neck!" he added, shouting after the boy.

Once they were aboard the camel again, Tarif squinted up at the sun, scanned the horizon, and pointed wordlessly at some landmark wholly invisible to MacLeod. The Scot shrugged, tapped the camel's neck, and they set off again, with what breeze as remained at their backs.

"MacLeod, tell me again about snow . . . ?"

Three hours later, the sun was near its zenith, and Duncan was beginning to wonder about the well ibn Ashraf had mentioned. It might take longer than he'd estimated, considering their need to stop for the vagaries of the weather. Pulling the camel to a halt, he asked, "How much farther?"

Tarif, perched behind him, shrugged. "Maybe one, two more miles, that way." He pointed to a ridge running perpendicular to their line of travel.

"You're sure about that?" One or two miles would be twenty minutes, perhaps. "There's water there?"

"Yes. Much water." In the emptiness of the rocky hills, the sound of creaking saddle leather, of cloth sliding against cloth as he looked around, was very loud. The camel snorted. Tarif started to ask another question, but MacLeod raised a hand to silence him.

Duncan took a deep breath and listened. The wind blew toward the ridge, but there was—something. A rumbling perhaps; a murmuring. He glanced skyward, and noted with a sense of foreboding the solitary vulture circling high over the ridge.

"Well then," he said resignedly, "let's go."

Chapter Twenty

<hr/>

We Watch. And we wait.

—Rebekah

The path into the mountains was becoming progressively more difficult. The fourth time the camel stumbled, Tarif remarked, "Soon we will have to leave her and go on foot."

"Oh, really?" MacLeod muttered, having come to the same conclusion at least an hour before. "Maybe one, two miles" had turned into four or ten or thirty. "And is there a good place to do that?"

"Soon. The last oasis is very close."

Since "very close" could mean "two weeks," Duncan was not sanguine about the possibilities. He had not thought it was possible that there could be a landscape less hospitable than the deep Nefud, but this one certainly challenged it for the title: a wilderness of red rock, split by time, erosion, the roots of bravely struggling shrubs. They were venturing deeper and deeper into a labyrinth.

He was shocked, therefore, to round the corner and find greenery. Where water came to the surface, there were trees, even some grass—and a Rolls Royce Blue Mist which had been most sadly mistreated. It was so out of place he stopped the camel and simply stared openmouthed.

Tarif peered around his shoulder. "What is that?" he said.

"It's an automobile." He attempted to urge the camel forward. The animal had no more experience with motor vehicles than the boy, and no desire to make a closer acquaintance. Finally Tarif slid off, ducked the shying animal, and ran over, to stop a few feet away, one finger creeping up to his mouth.

By dint of circling around the oasis, Duncan managed to find a place where the camel could not see, at least, the offending mass of metal. Still unhappy, the animal refused to settle, and his rider had to jump to the ground and tie the beast before going off to see for himself. There was, he noted, no one else at the little spring, though there was considerable sign of recent occupancy by man and, perhaps less recently, of horse. And then, of course, there was the car.

Tarif had not moved. Duncan patted him on the shoulder and went over to inspect the vehicle. The engine was as cool as anything metal could get in that sunlight, but the film of dust beginning to blossom on the exterior and lavish leather interiors was still thin. It had not been parked there long.

The engine turned over easily. Tarif yelped in surprise at the noise, and over on the other side of the oasis, behind the trees, the camel bellowed. Duncan let the engine idle for a few moments, enjoying the purr of good machinery, and then let it die.

"So the Rushallah guard Petra, do they?" he remarked ironically to the boy. "Seems I'm not the only unbeliever hereabouts."

"This is an Irzed well," Tarif said. His eyes were still as big as saucers. "What does it *do*?"

MacLeod looked from the vehicle to the boy and back again. Irzed. Another small detail no one had thought to mention. "Well, it moves," he answered finally. "Very fast, too, except . . ." gazing critically at one rear tire which had gone flat—"this one has gone lame. You've seen trains?"

Tarif shook his head blankly.

"Railroad tracks? You know, those lines of metal that cross the desert?"

Those he knew, and nodded vigorously.

"Well, this thing is related to those lines of metal." It might not be a relationship that made sense, but at least it would help the boy associate the thing with something with which he was familiar—or so Duncan hoped.

He was more concerned with the driver of the vehicle. The only reason he could imagine for it to be here, in the middle of the mountains, far from anything resembling a road, was that someone of comparative sophistication wanted to transport something that couldn't be conveniently conveyed by mule or camel. Say, the contents of the legendary vaults of Petra. Which meant that if he were to find anything worthwhile to bring to ibn Ashraf, he'd best be about it. He was beginning to think this place was far too popular.

"How far from here to Petra?"

Tarif, who had found the courage to actually come up to the car and touch it, and was busy running his hands over every square inch of the exterior, barely glanced at him. "Not far."

Duncan let go an explosive breath. "How far is 'not far' this time? In sun time, Tarif?"

Tarif squinted at the sky and held his fingers an inch or so apart, then went back to his explorations.

About two hours, then. It wasn't bad. "Let's go, then."

"Make it sing again," Tarif said. He was nerving himself for yet another step forward, and as Duncan watched, he leaped over the door and onto the seat beside him. "Make it sing!"

"Not now. When we come back, perhaps."

"I want to hear it sing now!"

Duncan turned in his seat and glared. Tarif slowly gave ground, clearly unhappy.

"The faster you show me the way, the sooner we'll be back here, and then perhaps you can hear it sing again." *Unless the rightful owner shows up*, he amended silently. Tarif sulked, but followed him out of the car, reluctantly.

The entrance to the canyon was no different, to MacLeod's eyes, than dozens of other shallow cracks in the red rock. Even Tarif had hesitated, making at least one false start, before choosing the opening in the mountain walls.

Somewhat to MacLeod's surprise, the passageway didn't dead-end, as the other had; the sheer walls rose on either side, keeping the floor of the little canyon in permanent chill and shadow. Four men could hold off an army here, he thought, as long as no one climbed up and dropped rocks on their heads. Looking upward to find a strip of blue sky was enough to make him dizzy; the cliffs seemed to lean inward. At several points he could extend his arms and touch both walls at once. If it were not for the traces of cut stone beneath his feet, showing that once, the way had been paved, he would have been certain they were completely lost. But even that was broken, cracked, and uncertain, and he had to be careful of his footing in the rubble.

He was more occupied with making sure where he was putting his feet than with looking ahead of himself, so when the sunlight splashed across his face, he looked up in surprise.

And caught his breath in sheer awe.

There before him, not twenty feet away, rising fifty feet high, carved out of the living rock, was the entrance to a temple, or perhaps a tomb. He had seen nothing to compare to it, not even among the ruins of the pharaohs; though if the pharaohs had had Greek architects, their resting places might have looked like this.

Columns. Carving, birds and animals. Delicate and massive and breathtaking, all carved into the coral sandstone cliff.

He had to crane his neck to see it; there was no way to get the proper perspective from the floor of the canyon. The edifice was easily a hundred feet long. In the sunlight, the stone almost glowed.

And it was old; old. Some of the carving, the details of the animals, the definition of the steps leading to the interior, had eroded away under the pressure of time and wind. But the columns, the cornices and domes and cupolas and arches and parapets, were still glorious. He moved forward as if under a spell, trying to see it all, and as he did so he caught sight of yet another building carved into a cliff across the valley.

The sight of it pulled him along the path that curved around the edge of the first temple—or perhaps it was a tomb—and as he followed it he saw, at last, Petra.

The whole valley had been turned into a city, not in the middle of the valley but carved into the red cliffs that defined it. It glowed in the sunlight: the "rose-red city, half as old as time."

An ancient king, it was said, had enslaved a hundred djinn, and they had labored a hundred years, carving the face of the cliffs into a glorious city of homes and temples and final resting places. Every surface seemed to be covered, some barely in bas-relief, some nearly freestanding.

He turned to find Tarif, to exclaim to him and point out the wonders to him, but the boy was still standing nearly invisible in the shadow of the crack in the cliffs, watching him. "Tarif!" he called.

Tarif . . . Tarif . . . Tarif . . .

The name echoed from cliff to cliff, from parapet to tower, startling him into reaching for the hilt of his sword. The boy backed away, not in fear of MacLeod but in sheer unease at the silent crimson city. As he did so, an uneasiness touched MacLeod, and he suddenly regretted the shout.

Somewhere in these mountains had to be the people who had driven that car.

Somewhere close.

From a window carved in the face of a cliff across the valley, al'Zafir and Aziz Bey, their attention seized by the echoes of a name, watched Duncan MacLeod pivoting, scanning the cliff faces with a watchfulness that had nothing to do with architectural appreciation.

"What is he looking for?" Aziz Bey asked irritably. "And what's he doing here anyway?"

"Perhaps the same thing you are, effendi," al'Zafir answered absentmindedly, fingering the hilt of his scimitar, a delighted smile hovering on his bearded lips. He backed away from the window opening as MacLeod turned in their direction. They were too far away to sense each other as Immortals, but movement could still be seen if they weren't careful. "The djinn will find him, I think."

"Why are you smiling like that? . . . I thought you didn't believe in djinn." Aziz Bey took one nervous step backward, out of the slant of sunlight through the windows.

"I do not fear them," al'Zafir corrected. "So, then. What you seek is not here, either?"

Aziz Bey glanced around the stone room. "No. Not here." He glared at his guide. The fellow was too disingenuous in his ignorance. "You said you knew this place. You told my father you knew where the treasure was."

"Ah, well." Al'Zafir shrugged. "I brought you here, did I not? Shall we go and ask the stranger whether he knows?"

Aziz shook his head stubbornly, then paused. "No, I don't want to ask him. But follow him, yes. Perhaps he does know better than you do. It wouldn't be difficult." An instant later he regretted the pettiness of the last remark, as al'Zafir turned that strange luminous smile on him, too.

"From a safe distance, yes, we can follow," he said. "And I think it is a good plan. We will find what we seek. All of us," he added softly.

His hand had never left the hilt of his sword.

MacLeod woke to find that he had slept the night through, and it was morning again. For a moment he was confused, and then remembered where he was, and what he was doing there.

Rolling onto his side, MacLeod propped up his head on one hand and looked over at the great entrance hall, still wondering at the incongruity of it, buried here in the mountains south of the Dead Sea. He had wanted to make camp inside the temple itself, but Tarif flatly refused to go farther than the portico of any of the buildings. Finally they had built a fire on a small rise near a spring, where they could look over most of the abandoned city and MacLeod could keep watch. He hadn't seen or heard any sign of others. He and Tarif might have been exploring a ghost city.

The rising sun made the carved walls glow pink and gold, catching the light, casting the night away as shadows that shortened as the sun climbed the sky. He watched for a few minutes, enthralled, and then rolled to his feet and stretched.

It had been too long, he decided, since he had gone through the rituals of the kata—several days at least. He had neglected them while he stayed with the Rushallah, but he couldn't afford to forgo them for very long, even here in the wilderness. Breathing deeply, he began with a formal salute to the rising sun, and then flowed into the smooth controlled violence of the prescribed movements, with and without the katana; shift, strike, parry, feint, one blending into the next without pause, without hesitation. After so long, so many, many years, his body knew the patterns without prompting.

When he had finished, and the sweat evaporating from his body left him shivering, he had found his center again. Finishing the exercise with a final, graceful salute, he turned to see Tarif watching him, eyes wide.

"Good morning," he said.

The boy flinched.

"What's wrong?" MacLeod asked, wiping the remains of the sweat from his torso and donning his thobe. Rummaging in the packs, he found a meager supply of hard bread and coffee. He had set water from the spring to boil before the boy, who was still watching his every move, found the courage to answer him.

"I thought you had been seized by djinn," he whispered, breaking the bread into successively smaller pieces. "What were you doing?"

MacLeod chuckled. "Ah, it was only stretching. Moving. Getting the blood to flow." The exercise had left him feeling good. He was prepared to deal with the occupants of the car, if they were really in the city; he was beginning to doubt it. There'd been no sign at all. But if they were around, it would make no difference; there had only been one car, after all. Either the vaults of Petra were empty, or there would be enough for all of them. He had hopes of finding the fabled vault, of coming away with some trinket overlooked by tomb robbers, bringing it triumphantly to ibn Ashraf, and actually completing his mission. And then, God willing, he could go back to Cairo. And from there, Europe; and perhaps even back to America. Anything seemed possible in the cool of the morning, deep in the mountains, drinking coffee in the empty plazas of an enchanted city.

"Where now d'you say this vault of yours is supposed to be, then?" he asked, his gaze skimming the parapets of the cliff houses as he sipped. Tarif still refused to enter any of the buildings. MacLeod missed his incessant chatter. It made the place seem even more quiet—perhaps it was only the scraping of the pan being replaced in the hot coals, set against the vast silence, that made it so. He was almost willing to swear he could hear the feathers of yon vulture stroking softly at the wind two hundred feet over their heads. And that tumbling rock, bouncing down the side of a cliff not too far away, was likely kicked loose by some invisible wild thing—

"Have a care for where you put your feet, you great oaf," Aziz snapped. "Do you want him to know we're here?" The two were crouched just within the shelter of a curve of rock, peering over the edge of a collapsed wall at the little camp across the canyon from them. The Turk didn't wait for an answer. "A man and a child—tomb robbers, no doubt. I could pick them off from here." He unholstered his pistol and started to bring it up.

The movement was stopped by an iron grip on his wrist. "No," al'Zafir ordered. "Let them find your treasure first. Then we will see about killing."

"What makes you think they can find it? We've been looking for days."

Al'Zafir shrugged. "They are more eyes to look. If they find it, we will take it from them."

"But we'll have to be closer."

Al'Zafir glanced out the opening again. "It is so—" he murmured thoughtfully. "Very well. Since you know best what it is you seek, effendi, go you quietly and creep close. I will follow after, and if you are discovered I can come to your aid."

"Are you mad? Did you see? The man had a bloody great *sword*!"

"But the effendi has a *gun*. It should be quite . . . safe." Al'Zafir gave the words just enough of a twist to speak volumes about Aziz's manhood.

The other man drew breath to protest, and then let it go again. "Very well," he agreed, and made his way to the staircase in the back of the room.

Al'Zafir looked out the window again at the man and boy, and licked his lips, and smiled again.

Chapter Twenty-one

*The English wish me to remain patient; they believe
MacLeod will return. My lord says the grazing is too
little here, and we must go on to the next oasis; he
does not think we will take any part in the wars the
great ones of this world wage.*

I wonder if I will hear anything more of MacLeod.
—Rebekah

"Well, do you at least know where the vaults are supposed to
be?" Duncan asked patiently as he entered the sunlight from
yet another building. He couldn't force the child to enter the
buildings, not when he was so obviously afraid.

"In the lesser temple," Tarif said uncertainly. "Or so
Ahmed's grandfather said."

That left open, of course, the question of exactly which
tomb was "the lesser" one. The first building, which faced
the narrow entrance to the valley, was almost completely
empty, save for small piles of debris and dry bones blown
into corners—the locals must have gotten to it before the
djinn took over, MacLeod thought, amused. Animals had
denned here, leaving tracks in the dust, but he had found no

human sign. He was beginning to believe the car's occupants had gotten lost in the mountains and never made it to Petra.

Putting together torches from some long-burning wood, he explored as far into other edifices nearby as he could. They had been chiseled quite deep into the cliff, and made clever use of windows. He thought the original inhabitants might have used reflectors, too, to illuminate the interiors, but they like everything else had been stripped away. After several hours' wandering from room to empty, high-vaulted room, he came out again, to find Tarif huddled disconsolately in the sunshine beside a dead fire. The boy greeted him with a completely uncharacteristic hug.

"Well, there's nothing there," he said, after setting the boy back on his feet and building up the fire for more coffee. "Do you remember anyone saying anything about what the place looked like?"

"It was red," Tarif said helpfully.

Duncan glanced around at the scarlet stone of the surrounding landscape. "A little more than that, if you can," he said wryly. "It all seems to be red in this place. Did he say anything else?"

The boy screwed up his face in a parody of effort to remember. "Ahmed said his grandfather had shot a djinn who lived in a round ball on top of the temple," he offered at last. "Maybe you could look for its body?"

Duncan pushed a piece of bread into his mouth, quickly surveying their supplies. Rope, yes. An extra knife was always handy. More than that could wait until he knew better what he was dealing with; more than that might require another trip. "I doubt after all this time it would still be there," he said gravely. "But we could look. Come on. . . . We'll stay on the path," he added, to reassure the child. Tarif bit his lip, and his hand crept into MacLeod's larger one as they walked.

It gave him another chance to look around, anyway. As the two of them walked along they pointed out items of interest to each other—fallen rocks, a snake, a finely carved pattern in the stone. They were halfway through the city when Tarif remarked, "Maybe Hamza doesn't want you to find his sword."

"Who? Why would Hamza—" Duncan stopped himself. "Oh, come now. Hamza el Kahir? You don't really believe Hamza's sword is here. He died far away from here."

Tarif gave him a wary look. "Have we not said so? Ibn Ashraf said you would bring him the Giver of Mercy, the Daughter—"

"—of Justice. Of course," MacLeod took a deep breath. It occurred to him suddenly that there was often some truth to legends. "You're certain?"

"Yes."

"Bloody hell." The words were in English. The sentiment was unmistakable.

Tarif shrugged. "I thought you knew." They passed another of the great temples. Tucked in behind it, in a fold of the cliff, was another, smaller edifice, like the one at the mouth of the canyon, only in miniature—the columns of the facade were only twenty-five feet tall. Over the doorway and down each side was a frieze of flowers and animals, supporting a peaked roof and framing the door. The two stopped to admire it.

"It is broken," Tarif declared. "So the angels treat all idolatry."

"Broken?" Duncan's eyes narrowed thoughtfully. Indeed, there was a granite ball at the peak of the roof, or rather part of one. Pieces had cracked off and lay scattered on the paving stones at their feet. "What idolatry?—oh, the pictures." Studying the pattern of flowers, he looked up at the broken ball. "I wonder just how adventurous Ahmed's grandfather was."

As he moved closer to the facade, Tarif glanced behind himself uneasily. When he brought his attention back to MacLeod, the Scot was halfway up the side of the building, climbing the pattern of flowers and vines.

"What are you doing, effendi?"

"Nothing any self-respecting goat wouldn't," MacLeod responded through his teeth. The sandstone was gritty beneath his fingertips. He wasn't looking down. Ahmed's grandfather had fallen. It followed that he must have fallen *from* something. It couldn't hurt to look, and the carvings invited a climb.

With a grunt, MacLeod heaved himself up onto the slanted roof—and promptly toppled behind it. The facade was only that—a facade. Behind it was a narrow alley, running parallel to the face of the building along its top, and a door in the face of the cliff, standing ajar.

"Effendi?" Tarif's call was high-pitched with anxiety.

"I'm all right, Tarif. I'll be—this may take a few minutes."

The dust indicated it had been a long while—maybe decades, but not more than that—since the door had been opened wide. MacLeod sneezed as he shoved it aside and blinked at the veils raised in the sunlight.

The reflector here was still in place.

The reflection illuminated the interior of a room perhaps twenty feet on a side. It was stacked to the ceiling with boxes, chests, and bales, all covered with gray dust, red sand, and spiderwebs. MacLeod sneezed again.

Most of the material had rotted into gauze. Waving spiderwebs out of his face, he pulled aside a carelessly flung robe—embroidered, once, with jewels that clattered to the floor and rolled into the corner as the cloth disintegrated—to reveal a waist-high chest.

The colors painted on the wood were still fresh and sharp after God only knew how long—blue and red and gold and black, arabesques and scrolls and patterns, flowers and gazelles and hunting lions and foxes. The covering had protected it from the dust; the spiders, from insects. Still, he lifted the lid carefully. The wax that had been used to seal it dissolved into white dust at his feet.

Inside were more boxes of all sizes, from small enough to present a lady's engagement ring to large enough for—a sword.

The brass-hinged brown box lying in the back of the chest drew his eyes like a magnet. It was exactly the size of a sword case. Could it really be Hamza's sword? How could Hamza's sword come here?

He pulled the case free and opened it.

It lay in a bed of disintegrating satin, the silver hilt black with tarnish. There was no way of knowing how it had come here, more than a thousand miles from the blood-soaked sands of Algiers; but the blue steel still gleamed even in the reflected light, and he could still trace the inscription, placed there by a good man with a dignified sense of humor, an Immortal who had died too young: the veritable scimitar of Hamza el Kahir.

There might be other things here that ibn Ashraf could use to demonstrate his tribe's wealth and generosity to Faisal ibn Hussein, but this sword, which had sunk deep into his own flesh centuries ago, he wanted for himself. He replaced it reverently in the case and carried it outside.

"Tarif!"

The boy was looking over his shoulder again, as if expecting a djinni to creep up behind him. He jumped at the sound of his name.

"Tarif, I have found it. I'm going to lower this to you. Come and catch it as it comes down."

The boy didn't want to. He kept looking back, down to the inner city of Petra. MacLeod finished rigging a sling and looped the rope around the base of the broken ball—the father of Ashraf was a barbarian to use such a thing for target practice. "Tarif, come on. The faster you help me, the quicker we'll be out of here."

It was an argument that made sense. The boy ran forward as Duncan lowered the sword case, wincing every time it scraped against the sandstone columns. Finally it rested safely in the child's arms. "Stay there," he instructed. "I'll be right back."

Before Tarif had a chance to say anything, Duncan turned to go back into the vault. One more thing, something striking the Rushallah sheikh could—

Tarif screamed.

MacLeod was out the door and snatching a quick glance over the parapet before the echoes had died away from the rose-red walls. That glance was enough to meet the gaze of the man in the Turkish uniform and red fez holding a gun to the child's head, looking up and grinning. The sword case lay open at the boy's feet, the blade inside lit by direct sunlight for the first time in centuries. Duncan blinked in surprise, startled. The Turk was not an Immortal, but like Tarif, he would be, one day.

"Come down, you Bedu thief," the Turk called pleasantly. "And bring me a gift while you do so, and perhaps the boy will live."

"What kind of gift?" MacLeod yelled back, listening to the rough edges of his Arabic being lost in the distorting echoes. His hand went automatically to the hilt of the katana; he had to force himself to take the pistol instead. "There is great treasure here. Gold, jewels. Enough for both of us. Leave the boy out of it."

"The boy is my surety for your good behavior. Come down!"

He was not about to encumber himself with anything more from the vault, but he had to have a way to disguise the gun. The cloth in the treasure room was too rotten. Finally, exasperated, he took the kaffiyeh from his head, stuffed the agal into a pocket, and draped the cloth around the weapon. Standing up slowly, he held the "package" high.

"What is it?"

"You'll have to wait until I have the boy," he replied with more confidence than he felt. He saw the start of amazement as the Turk realized he was no Arab, and smiled grimly to himself: the man had more surprises than that awaiting him. He started to clamber over the side of the parapet, holding on to both ends of the rope and hoping the base of the broken ornament was strong enough to take his weight, when the awareness of the presence of another Immortal came to him.

There. Coming up the path from the inner city, an Immortal. Not a boy like Tarif, not like this pudgy, soft Turk; a Bedouin, a fighter, coming with his hand upon the hilt of his sword, lowering the fold of his headcloth to reveal his face, his pleased grin. He knew that grin.

"We meet again. Did I not say it, Frank?"

Duncan slid down the rope, nearly forgetting about the pistol in his hands in the need to take up his sword. But if the Turk shot him, he'd be dead just long enough to lose his head. He needed the Turk out of the way long enough to deal with the Immortal, but he needed to get Tarif away from the Turk first.

"I told you I would take your head," al'Zafir said pleasantly. "It is time, Duncan MacLeod."

Chapter Twenty-two

"We are in public," Duncan said between his teeth. "Let the boy go."

"These?" The other Immortal laughed. "They are our kin."

Both the Turk and the boy looked confused at this.

"I don't want to get involved in your petty quarrels," the Turk shouted. "I want—I want something." He stopped, frustrated by his ability to be more specific. "All you've brought is an old, useless sword. I want something more! Something beautiful!"

"A sword?" The word caught al'Zafir's interest. "Let me see." He came up to the Turk and jerked the boy out of the way as if he were so much old clothing, sending him sprawling across the path. The Turk sputtered with rage, raising the gun to his former guide, who was lifting the "old sword" from the case with considerable reverence.

MacLeod didn't have the energy to spare in outrage at how Tarif had been treated. He gave him one look, indicating the path back to the canyon with his eyes, and then snapped his focus back to the two adults, hoping Tarif had the sense to take the hint. A scramble of rocks managed to reassure him.

That left two of them—one bearing mortal death, the other, Immortal.

"You fool," al'Zafir was saying. "Can you not see?" He was stroking the blade of the sword with gentle fingers.

The Turk lowered his gun, momentarily, in order to look. " 'I am made at the hand of Hamza ibn Mohammed Yaman al Katib al Khal', in the name of the Merciful, the Compassionate, blessed be He forever and ever; I am the Giver of Mercy, the Drinker of the Blood of Infidels, the Taker of Heads, the Daughter of Justice.'

"This? *This* is the Daughter of Justice, the scimitar of el Kahir?" The Turk was incredulous.

"Yes," al'Zafir exulted. He raised it high. "See how it honors you, my kinsman?"

The scimitar sliced down, across the Turk's belly, and the man staggered backward, the fez rolling across the paving stones into the shadows cast by the cliffs in the late-afternoon sun. He screamed as blood gushed from his body and writhed on the ground, his movements weaker and weaker as he died.

"He will be a pretty taste for after," al'Zafir said, turning to MacLeod with the same engaging smile. "And then I shall see about the little one. I have not yet decided what I will do about him."

"He is only a boy," MacLeod said, furious.

"He is one of us," al'Zafir pointed out. "Let him learn the way of the sword. Meanwhile, you and I have a matter between us, Duncan MacLeod. I told you I would come for you with a weapon worthy of your own."

The lengthening shadows of the deep canyon were deceptive, treacherous. There was no ideal time and place, of course, but these were far from being his preferred conditions to fight for his head—for his life. The footing was bad—the shadow could be merely a shadow, or it could be a hole to catch and twist and bring him down.

They were outside the precincts of the temple, if temple it

was; outside of forbidden, holy ground. He discarded the pistol—it would be easy merely to shoot the other man and then take his head, but it was not honorable; not his way. He drew the dragon-headed katana, standing at guard. "I am here."

Al'Zafir laughed. "I see our little brother has come back," he remarked, using the tip of his sword to point to a jumble of rocks at the lip of the canyon.

Duncan didn't make the elementary error of looking in the direction the other man pointed. He didn't need to; a shadow deeper than other shadows stirred, watching. Duncan held back a curse; the boy was a distraction he didn't need just now—

"Tarif!" His voice was rough with anxiety. "Tarif, listen to me. Go back to the Rushallah. Go to ibn Ashraf." If al'Zafir won this fight, he would go after the child next. With luck, the sheikh could protect him—but MacLeod no longer believed in that kind of luck.

Tarif made an inarticulate sound of protest.

Al'Zafir laughed and leaped forward, a long black shadow reaching for the boy. Duncan flowed to intercept him. Tarif, correctly interpreting the upraised weapons, scuttled backwards and disappeared down a turn in the narrow canyon. Without the slightest pause, MacLeod and al'Zafir changed objectives, and the swords rang together.

Duncan feinted to his right, trying to force the other man to circle so the fast-fading sunlight would be in his face and Duncan would have the slight advantage of shadow. Al'Zafir ignored the feint and brought the ancient sword up in a wicked slash, sending the Turk's blood flying from its edge across MacLeod's face.

The katana slapped around as if with a will of its own and met the other man's sword edge to edge; they slid off each other with a shriek like demons, and the two stood back and circled warily.

The katana was longer, giving Duncan a few inches of vital reach on the other man. Al'Zafir was fast, though, very fast, and used the doubtful light to good advantage. He had a tendency to cut instead of thrust, and Duncan spent a busy few moments blocking a flurried attack, using the time to take the measure of his opponent.

"I will add your sword to my collection as well," the Arab said conversationally, in the short pause before launching another attack. "Tell me its name and its history before you die, so it will not be forgotten."

Duncan grunted. A fight was business, not an occasion for witty repartee; besides, the other man hadn't waited for a response, but had instead launched another attack. Duncan beat it off and countered, but al'Zafir faded back, leading him into a particularly rocky area of the disintegrating pavement. The Arab stumbled, and the katana swept down, but the Arab blocked it and rolled away.

He fought well in the robes, Duncan noted, wishing absently that he could shed the damned things himself. At least a kilt was decently short; this long gown had a tendency to tangle around his ankles, making him wary of trying to duck and roll for fear he wouldn't be able to get up again.

"Is your sword nameless then?" al'Zafir taunted. "Has it no honor, no fame?" He attacked again, and shifted his line midmotion; Duncan moved aside, but not quite enough. A line of red marked his sleeve.

It was hardly a serious cut—only a graze, really—but it was enough to stain the cloth before it healed itself. And it stung. "You're a fine one to talk about honor," MacLeod snarled. "Calling a man kin, and murdering him. You'd take a man's head before the man ever has a chance to learn the rules, much less how to defend himself? I call that a coward's way—"

"I call it a survivor's way." Al'Zafir smiled. "And that is

the first rule of all, is it not? And for that reason"—the swords clashed again, raising sparks, and the two men came together corps a corps, until al'Zafir was grinning in Duncan's face—"I am absolved—"

They stumbled apart, and a rock rolled under Duncan's foot, sending him staggering backward, off balance.

If it had happened at any other time, he would have been in serious trouble. As it was, his opponent barely checked himself from following him up and plunging the sword between his ribs, immobilizing him long enough to take his head. He was looking past MacLeod, an odd, bemused expression on his face.

It was the oldest trick in the book, but this time MacLeod risked a rapid glance behind him.

It was the Turk, standing up again, one hand at his belly, a look of horror on his face, and the gun in his hand wavering between al'Zafir and MacLeod. He took three unsteady steps forward and cocked the revolver. They were too close together. Too close. Al'Zafir came forward; Duncan couldn't tell who was his target, himself or the Turk.

It was against all the rules for one Immortal to interfere in a duel between two others, but the Turk was too young, too new to know about Rules; he might not even realize he had come back from death. He stepped between them even as al'Zafir's sword rose.

There was no time to explain, to push the Turk away, to do anything but defend himself or die. MacLeod took the dragon hilt in both hands, rose, and whirled in one continuous movement.

The katana, capable of cutting through iron, went through al'Zafir's neck easily. MacLeod tried to check the killing swing before it could claim the Turk's head as well, but the momentum was too much. Two heads fell, two Quickenings rose. The Turk's, a mere crackle, a hint of what the man might have been—and then al'Zafir's power swept down on him.

When the darkness was over, and the lightning, the small boy crept out of the canyon to see what remained of the Frankish effendi. The red sandstone temple, with its vault of treasures, had been reduced to a pile of rubble from the fight outside its precincts. What was left were only the swords, three of them; and of the combatants, only one.

Chapter Twenty-three

No Watcher had written of what went on in the city of Petra, much to Joe Dawson's disgust. The only record lay in the continuing nightmares of the boy Tarif, as recorded by the Watcher Rebekah in the tribe of the Rushallah. MacLeod had come back with the boy and with the legendary sword of el Kahir, and turned it over to the Rushallah sheikh, who had in turn presented it to Faisal ibn Hussein. Shortly afterward, MacLeod had vanished, to reappear in the European theatre driving an ambulance.

Al'Zafir ibn Muhunnad had disappeared permanently. No great loss, as Dawson recalled. It seemed possible his path might have crossed MacLeod's and terminated abruptly.

Tarif, as Dawson recalled, had lived another dozen or so years and then been killed in some bizarre accident or other; he'd been lucky, finding a teacher fairly quickly. He could check the records and find out who his Watcher was and where he was living now. He didn't think the boy had crossed MacLeod's path since. He might have, of course. Perhaps Tarif was the source of the reappearance of Hamza's sword; perhaps he himself might reenter MacLeod's life. Stranger things had happened.

For all the efforts of the Watchers, there would always be holes in the Chronicles; so long as the Watchers remained secret, held themselves aloof, they would never be entirely successful.

But he was lucky, he realized suddenly; he could always ask his subject what had happened in the city of Petra, in the winter of 1916–17. And if the Immortal was so inclined, he might even tell him.

He had some interesting conversations in front of him, he thought, lifetimes of them. He raised his cup in a silent toast to the memory of Hamza el Kahir, and to the generations of Watchers who had preceded him. He hoped they'd be listening.